George Barnett Smith

Shelley

A Critical Biography

George Barnett Smith

Shelley
A Critical Biography

ISBN/EAN: 9783743313330

Manufactured in Europe, USA, Canada, Australia, Japa

Cover: Foto ©Raphael Reischuk / pixelio.de

Manufactured and distributed by brebook publishing software
(www.brebook.com)

George Barnett Smith

Shelley

SHELLEY

A CRITICAL BIOGRAPHY

BY

GEORGE BARNETT SMITH

AUTHOR OF 'POETS AND NOVELISTS,' ETC.

EDINBURGH

DAVID DOUGLAS

1877

I INSCRIBE

THIS LITTLE VOLUME

TO MY WIFE.

CONTENTS.

I.—SHELLEY'S EARLIER YEARS.

CONTENTS.

CONTENTS.

IV.—THE POETRY OF SHELLEY.

V.—THE POETRY OF SHELLEY—*Concluded.*

I.

SHELLEY'S EARLIER YEARS.

" Fearless he was, and scorning all disguise,
  What he dared do or think, though men might start,
  He spoke with mild yet unaverted eyes;

  Liberal he was of soul, and frank of heart,
  And to his many friends—all loved him well—
  Whate'er he knew or felt he would impart,

  If words he found those inmost thoughts to tell ;
  If not, he smiled or wept ; and his weak foes
  He neither spurned nor hated—though with fell

  And mortal hate their thousand voices rose,
  They passed like aimless arrows from his ear."
                                    Prince Athanase.

I.

SHELLEY'S EARLIER YEARS.

THE poetic revival witnessed at the dawn of the nineteenth century came from opposite sides. Its music and its passion were typified in Shelley, and its devotion to nature in Wordsworth. These poets were the antithesis of the classical school represented by Dryden and Pope, men who were moulded by, and did not mould, their age. I take Shelley and Wordsworth as exponents of the new order, because Byron, though uniting, in an inferior degree, the qualities of both, did not, in the general outline of his genius, distinctively set forth the special and distinguishing characteristics of either. Shelley rebelled against organised society, and poured his wrath and his ecstasies into his verse; Wordsworth, touched into a noble frame of mind by the initiation of the French Revolution, saw as in a vision the grand triumph of right over might in the immediate distance. The aristocrat

B

and the plebeian—Shelley was the descendant of
two illustrious families, and Wordsworth was the
son of a country attorney—early in life indulged
the same sanguine political aspirations.   Both
were Republicans and Communists in spirit, inspired, in the outset, by the grand idea of hastening
that period when the brotherhood of man should
be recognised throughout the world.   Working in
different grooves, they likewise effected a revolution
in poetic literature.   Shelley—who by his family
connected himself with Sir Philip Sidney, the pure
and noble knight of immortal renown—never lost
his faith in those principles which filled his own
father with horror.   The dignity of man outweighed
with him all titular glories, and to the last this great
and unfortunate genius preserved his conscience
free of reproach, and loved his species after the most
shameful usage.   The enfranchisement of humanity
was with him a deeper sentiment than with Wordsworth.   The latter—whom we may assuredly regard as the equal of any English poet, save Milton
(whom also he excelled in certain aspects), since the
time of Shakspeare—had really Conservative instincts beneath the enthusiasm which welled up
within him at the thought of freedom being gained
for France.   Contentedly absorbed in the tranquil
beauty of nature, he was ultimately seized with

affright at the natural concomitants of that very Revolution which, in its inception, he hailed with so much ardour. The Reign of Terror dissipated his dream of universal happiness. Shelley, looking back to the Revolution, saw in it a necessary national purification. So much tyranny and wrong had been perpetrated for centuries, that he knew the balance could not be adjusted without blood. Far from possessing the mental equipoise of Wordsworth, he gazed further into the future than his fellow-poet, for the effects of the great Revolution—though in his own crusade against evil he worked with all the energy and impatience of the man who believes he can convert the world in a day. The Reign of Terror, which to many was but a brief yet terrible episode in a great upheaval, to Wordsworth was the complete overthrow of all his hopes, and transformed him into a Conservative. De Quincey, his friend, wrote in just rebuke of his want of faith at this crisis—"The Reign of Terror was a mere fleeting and transitional phasis. The Napoleon dynasty was nothing more. Even that very Napoleon scourge, which was supposed by many to have consummated and superseded the Revolution, has itself passed away upon the wind—has itself been superseded—leaving no wreck, no relic, or record behind, except precisely those changes which it worked, *not in its character of an enemy to the Revolution* (which also it was), *but as its servant and its tool.* See, even whilst we speak, the folly of that cynical sceptic who would not allow time for great natural processes of purification to travel onwards to their birth, or wait for the evolution of natural results: the storm that shocked him has wheeled away; the frost and the hail that offended him have done their office; the rain is over and gone; happier days have descended upon France; the voice of the turtle is heard in all her forests; once again, after two thousand years of serfdom, man walks with his head erect; Bastiles are no more; every cottage is searched by the golden light of law; and the privileges of religious conscience have been guaranteed and consecrated for ever and ever." Thirty years have passed since these words were written, and France has recently gone through stupendous throes, from which she has emerged with strong and erect presence; but the grandeur of her destiny is not yet accomplished. When we remember, however, the days of her darkness, has the price paid for her present position been too great? Wordsworth yearned for immediate fruition; but an idea sometimes takes a thousand years to acquire the concrete form of action.

I have been impelled to this comparison because

a fervent radicalism (which remains to be considered more fully) was one of the changeless ideas and convictions of Shelley. From his earliest years of thought we find it asserting itself, separating the poet from all the natural ties and . associations by which he was environed. To understand him fully he must be regarded in this light, viz., as one who, from the first moment of his intellectual consciousness, indulged an antipathy to many social institutions, while he loved and pitied the individual. As a child, his keen and weird imagination, teeming with vivid conceptions of the ideal, was not all that was noticeable in him. His thoughts and aspirations were not those of the rest of his schoolfellows, and he must be followed closely from the time when he first began to think and to suffer. His mind, even in its first evolutions, was busy with the Infinite. He was making daily excursions into the vast region of the unknown. His schoolfellows, being unable to comprehend him, busied themselves in tormenting him, and in endeavouring to render his life a burden. One can imagine how St. Augustine's language would apply to him, when he said that "the boy's sufferings while they last are quite as real as those of the man;" indeed, we may credibly suppose that his anguish was almost keener in these early days at

the injustice he endured than it was when oppro-
brious epithets were lavishly hurled at him in
after years. Verses which he subsequently wrote
show how completely isolated he was from those
whom he daily met *in statu pupillari*, and how even
at that period he was leading a separate existence,
like some lonely, melancholy star :—

> " I do remember well the hour which burst
> My spirit's sleep : a fresh May dawn it was,
> When I walk'd forth upon the glittering grass,
> And wept, I knew not why : until there rose
> From the near schoolroom voices that, alas !
> Were but one echo from a world of woes—
> The harsh and grating strife of tyrants and of foes.

> " And then I clasped my hands, and look'd around ;
> But none was near to mock my streaming eyes,
> Which poured their warm drops on the sunny ground :
> So, without shame, I spake :—' I will be wise,
> And just, and free, and mild, if in me lies
> Such power ; for I grow weary to behold
> The selfish and the strong still tyrannize
> Without reproach or check.' "

Remembering all that is implied in these lines,
and the facts upon which the description is based,
it is scarcely matter for wonder that Percy Bysshe
Shelley, the most spiritual of all the poets of the
nineteenth century, remains, in many aspects, one

of the unsolved problems of literature. Misapprehended and misunderstood, more perhaps than any other man of equal genius, by his own generation, even at this day also his name excites a visible tremor in those whose estimate of him has been formed from a superficial examination of his extraordinary character. The wild beauty of his song penetrates every mind which is capable of being moved by poetic thought and expression; yet from the moment when this grand but erratic luminary first shot across the horizon of English literature, readers and critics have been divided into two distinctly hostile camps whenever any attempt has been made to assign him his true position. We are in the habit of thinking that the poet is never happy till his death; but neither in his life nor since his death has the just balance been held with regard to Shelley—his detractors ever being unwilling to give due weight to the circumstances of his life, and his unreasoning admirers being blinded to his imperfections by the excess and magnificence of his poetic vision. More than most men in his art has he excited a personal interest in the legion of his commentators and elucidators, and in almost all that has been said of him some warp or bias is easily discernible. A curious and interesting study may, however, be made of this gifted being, if we examine, by the light of well-ascertained facts, the springs of thought and action in his early life—and it is a study which will materially assist towards a conception of the real nature of the poet in his later years. From the very youth of Shelley the inter-connection between sensation, fact, and action was so close and intimate—distinguishing in truth the whole of his strange and brilliant career—that the incidents of his history become necessary to a true understanding of his poetry and of his character. The poet lives in his emotions; pre-eminently was this the case with Shelley; and the singular strength and tenacity of his feelings will in a large measure account for the failure of mere criticism, unassisted by a quick sympathy, to arrive at a just estimate of the poet and the man. My present object is chiefly to set forth, as I conceive him, Shelley—while yet in his youth, through his genius and personality, —a being permeated with the "enthusiasm of humanity" to a degree seldom witnessed in recent generations. Biography will be an adjunct, by whose aid we shall endeavour to get at the soul of the poet, and to unravel some of those tangled threads of character which puzzle most students of his nature, and which have even betrayed men of kindred gifts into unworthy aspersions upon his.

name. For nearly two centuries past no more remarkable phenomenon has arisen—a phenomenon
at once so striking and so splendid—the terror of
those who saw in him only the fiery champion of
Atheism, but a glorious radiance to all who have
finally comprehended the efforts of his imagination
and the nobility of his heart. He can scarcely
pass for a true lover of poetry who has not in his
youth revelled in the luxuriant, if crude, fancies of
Queen Mab; nor, further, can he be said to have
done justice to strength of thought in his later age
except *The Cenci* and *Prometheus Unbound* have,
with other extraordinary creations, commanded his
willing admiration. This sanguine and rebellious
spirit had but one equal in his day—he to whom
I have already made reference—Wordsworth, the
patriarch of the North, who, filled with a calm as
majestic as that which possessed the mountains and
lakes of his inspiration, was in almost every respect the opposite of his younger brother in song.

One trembles for the veracity of history in
relation to past ages, when we remember how
circumstances which occurred only fifty years ago
have been distorted for the convenience of interested persons. Shelley, like Dr. Johnson, had
his Boswell, and the biographer of the former has
left behind him a work almost unique, vying with

the Scotsman's immortal record. But with this
qualifying adjective all similarity ends. Boswell
was content to narrate facts; but, when necessary
for his theories, Shelley's biographer is said to
have been prolific in inventing them. There would
be little difficulty in tracing many of the false conceptions of the poet's character to his door. The
invention of a fact, indeed, appears with him to
have been most easy of accomplishment. And if
other facts more trustworthy than his own proved
refractory, so much the worse for the opposing
facts; but these could not be allowed to deter him
for a moment in his development of the relations
between Shelley's work and his life. To prove that
the poet never conducted himself as other mortals
(even in his youth), a lengthy disquisition was
written upon Shelley's "raising the Devil" at
Oxford—not a formidable operation at any time, if
we are to believe the theologians, seeing that the
enemy of the human race is always close at our
elbow. Yet boyish pranks like this have been
solemnly paraded as affording a clue to the understanding of the poet, although every youth of
Shelley's ingenious mind and lively spirit exhibits
similar idiosyncrasies, upon which it would be absurd to build a serious and elaborate superstructure.
Then, again, this biographer—and he was not the

only untrustworthy biographer Shelley has had—
manifested an obvious political bias, and the opinions
of the poet, both religious and political, terribly
disturbed his equilibrium. In one passage Hogg
observes of his friend—"He gave himself up too
much to people who have since been called Radicals;
these were necessarily vulgar; they dreaded and detested his conspicuously aristocratical and gentle-
manlike dispositions, and being commonly needy
men, chiefly perhaps because they were lazy and dissipated, they preyed upon him most unmercifully."
The absurdity of this passage is only equalled by its
puerility; but it is very valuable as showing the
calibre of the man who undertook to tell us the story
of Shelley's life. His greatest condemnation lies in
the fact that the man of genius and the aristocrat
could be a Radical of the most advanced type.
Other biographers have given us details of their
respective friendships with Shelley, and, though
these are marked by errors, they are yet more
useful for the purposes of the student from the
fact that they are not disfigured by personal feelings and animosities. But the reflection still
recurs, how inadequate is all that has been written
to place in a just light in the eyes of posterity that
singular being whose genius was of so sublime and
transcendent an order. . Ample materials exist for

the construction of a complete biography, but obstacles still intervene to prevent the accomplishment of the task with the requisite fulness and freedom. "Pelion upon Ossa" is but a faint shadowing forth of the memorial volumes and editions of Shelley which have been issued; but many of these never had any *raison d'être* whatever, and they only serve to intensify our perplexity and bewilderment in endeavouring to consolidate the facts of Shelley's life. Perhaps the only solid rock in these drifting sands of biography is that volume wherein Lady Shelley has given us a brief memorial of her illustrious relative. Meanwhile, pending the publication of the full and complete history of Shelley, it is not impossible to advance a solution of many problems suggested by his career. And one of the questions we have to ask is, Will the poet yet be reconciled to the mass of human beings whose feelings De Quincey declared him to have outraged—not only in his own, but in every age—by his attack upon established dogma and religion ? I refuse, for one, to signify adhesion to De Quincey's view,—to believe that when Shelley's character is placed in a clearer light, he will still be regarded as the bitter enemy of all religious teaching and belief. In stating the grounds for this opinion, I shall not plead for his memory *ad. misericordiam*, but by right of that eternal justice which he was ever the first to invoke and acknowledge.

Before the childish principle of selfishness is usually eliminated from the breast, Shelley was troubled and perplexed by the wrongs and misery of the world. Yet never were divine pity and magnanimity crushed out of his soul. All the malignity of his foes, and all the suffering which fell to his lot, only served to make the flame of his noble philanthropy burn the brighter and with a purer radiance. Despotism never conquered the fresh feelings of his heart, and his gentleness seemed to grow by the unlikely meat it fed on. Of the strange schoolboy at Brentford, "nursing his mighty youth," unsuspected of genius, and apparently the bitter sport of fate, we have the following portraiture: "Shelley was slightly yet elegantly formed; he had deep blue eyes, of a wild, strange beauty, and a high white forehead, overshadowed with a quantity of dark-brown curling hair. His complexion was very fair; and, though his features were not positively handsome, the expression of his countenance was one of exceeding sweetness and sincerity. His look of youthfulness he retained to the end of his life, though his hair was beginning to get grey— the effect of intense study, and of the painful agitations of mind through which he had passed."[1] As the result of his endowments, though Shelley paid little attention to his tasks at school, he easily outstripped his companions. But the daily routine was singularly wearisome to him, and was rendered doubly so by the petty persecutions to which he was subjected, and which he regarded as very atrocious. This was one of the first intimations of his recognition of the dignity of the human soul, and of his unchangeable determination never to see it degraded in his own person. A strong antipathy to physical punishments was displayed when he visited his sister Helen at the school at Clapham, and insisted upon the cessation of what he considered to be a derogatory method of correction. Referring to his school life, one writer says, "I do not give him as an example for children to follow. Away with this cant of schoolboy reproving. I describe, and as far as in me lies unfold, the secrets of a human heart; and, if I be true to nature, I depict an uprightness of purpose, a generosity of sentiment, and a sweetness of disposition, that yielded not to the devil of hate, but to the God of love, unequalled by any human being that ever existed. Tamed by affec-

[1] Other portraits have been given of Shelley, but this description appears to be the most authentic.

tion, but unconquered by blows, what chance was there that Shelley should be happy at a public school?" It is strange that this man, who should have excited such an intense veneration in every individual who knew him personally, should have been subjected to bitter diatribes from those who ran with the multitude to condemn him, but who were utterly unable to comprehend his nature.

Shelley at Eton displayed that fearlessness of character which ever strongly distinguished him. He opposed with passionate ardour the system of fagging which was pursued, and his individual force was such that he kept down the hateful system, so far as he was personally concerned. As for the stories told of his residence, both here and at Oxford, are they not too familiar to need repetition? Doubtless, his eccentricities have been exaggerated; whilst his serious periods of reflection and isolation—during which his fruitful imagination conjured up strange visions, creating and peopling worlds—were taken as evidences that he was unsociable, if not morose. Probably the whole matter is a misconception. As well make oil and water coalesce as adapt Shelley to the moods of the youths with whom he was associated. Constantly rising to another sphere, he

was only occasionally brought down to actual
mundane affairs and persons. Yet that he was
capable of forming sincere and lasting friendships
has been abundantly proved. When a youth, his
large soul was impatient of everything paltry
and mean of which it could not avoid cognizance.
But the pleasures of his imagination were so strong
and satisfying as to draw him away largely from
ordinary communion with humanity. Then, too,
even in the days of boyhood, there were floating
in his mind certain undefined schemes which he
longed to promulgate for the amelioration of the
race; and there is something beautiful, if almost
grotesque, in the fact of a youth of seventeen being
so impressed with the necessity of working for the
good of his species, as to contemplate the issue
of a novel which was to give the death-blow to
intolerance. Concerning those anecdotes which
have sometimes been taken to point to incipient
madness, I need not say much. After carefully
examining them, nothing remains but what may
be attributed to a simple feverishness of the nerves.
Earnestness and restlessness—which never slept
till his body perished in the blue Mediterranean—
qualities whose permeating influences were peculiarly exceptional in him, made him seem a
being of another type. He experienced, also, but

only on two or three separate occasions in his
lifetime, peculiar visions or hallucinations, which
were probably the result of a surcharge of ideality,
and nothing more. But of many of his extraordinary deeds we should never have heard, had
he not developed into an unquestionably great
poet. When genius becomes manifest, it pays
the penalty of having all the trivial actions of
youth unearthed, and canvassed as remarkable
incidents, whose real import is now only discovered for the first time. Occasionally these incidents are invented. That Shelley was eccentric—
a being, that is, who does not move in the common
groove but who will have his own orbit—is an
undoubted fact; nor does it admit of denial that
his consciousness of divergence from the mental
constitution of others led him to isolate himself,
just as the early intimations of genius, so different
in kind, led to the seclusiveness of James Watt.

The fact that Shelley was called "Atheist" at
Eton has been held to be indicative of his opinions
thus early in life, although it has been pointed
out that the term Atheist was applied at Eton
to one who ventured to set even the temporal
authorities at defiance. Such speculations as these
are worthless in helping us to arrive at a judgment
upon the man. We are at a loss to know what

basis of truth exists in them, and it is as foolish as it is unjust to attempt to construct a theory of character when we are absolutely in doubt as to the preliminary steps being sound and undeniable. This much, and this only, is safely and legitimately deducible from Shelley's stay at Eton—that here was a remarkable youth, who could not possibly be confounded with the common herd; one whose vivid but confused imagination was struggling after divine forms in which to express itself; one who was the sworn foe of injustice, and who was prepared to combat it, even if the result involved martyrdom. But he was no Atheist as yet in the ordinary acceptation of the term. He undoubtedly hated all authority which did not spring from love; but upon distinctively religious and theological questions he had not yet begun to formulate his views. His idea of abolishing God, and conducting the world upon an improved principle, was reserved for a rather later stage of his existence.

There is strong ground for the conviction that the brief interregnum between Shelley's leaving Eton and his being entered at Oxford witnessed a great and noticeable expansion of his mind. This was the result of the freedom and solitariness which he enjoyed at home, where he busied himself deeply in learning and in various speculations. At any rate, when we next meet with him as an undergraduate of University College, it is to see one who bent himself to the studies which fell to his lot with an ardour that astonished those of less sanguine temperament. Several literary efforts which he put forth antecedent to this period really gave no adequate foreshadowing of his powers. Passing by a play which he wrote when a mere boy, in conjunction with his sister Elizabeth, and which probably merited no warmer appreciation than it received from the great comedian Mathews, we come to the *Wandering Jew*, a work, it is said, he wrote in conjunction with Medwin, but which in reality was altogether Shelley's own. Some biographers appear to have no knowledge of this effusion; but as a matter of fact, all its leading ideas were afterwards worked up by Shelley in his poems. For his first published work, *Zastrozzi*, a novel, Shelley received the sum of forty pounds; but this indiscretion of publication as regards Shelley does not appear to have been repeated by the publishers who issued the work. *Zastrozzi* was a mixture of the styles of Mrs. Radcliffe and Matthew Gregory Lewis, the latter being then a favourite author with Shelley; but a story written by Dr. Moore about a century ago must also have made some impression on the young author. Suffice it to say, that the novel

was a wild, if eloquent, absurdity ; and that probably the most satisfactory thing in connection with
it was a magnificent banquet which Shelley was
enabled to give to eight friends out of the proceeds
of the romance. Another work, written by Shelley
at a somewhat later date, *St. Irvyne*, was simply
the result of an extensive reading of weird tales and
novels, and only those persons who have a keener
insight than is to be obtained by fair criticism
could detect in it anything which would warrant its
republication. A volume to which more interest
attaches is that entitled *Original Poetry by Victor
and Cazire*. Stockdale, the publisher, gives the
following account of this volume and its principal
author :—" The unfortunate subject of these very
slight recollections introduced himself to me in the
autumn of 1810. He was extremely young. I
should think he did not look more than eighteen.
With anxiety in his countenance, he requested me
to extricate him from a pecuniary difficulty in
which he was involved with a printer, whose name
I cannot call to mind, but who resided at Horsham,
near to which Timothy Shelley, Esquire, afterwards,
I believe, made a baronet, the father of our poet, had
a seat called Field Place. I am not quite certain
how the difference between the poet and the
printer was arranged ; but, after I had looked over

the account, I know that it was paid, though whether I assisted in the payment by money or acceptance I cannot remember. The letters show that it was accomplished just before my too conscientious friendship caused our separation. Be that as it may, on the 17th of September, 1810, I received fourteen hundred and eighty copies of a thin royal 8vo volume, entitled *Original Poetry by Alonzo and Cazire*, or two names something like them. . The author told me that the poems were the joint production of himself and a friend, whose name was forgotten by me as soon as I heard it." Stockdale adds, that from these trifles which he published, and from personal intercourse, he at once formed an opinion that Shelley was not an every-day character. There are some speculations to the effect that Shelley's coadjutor in this volume was his cousin and first love, Miss Harriet Grove, who was on a visit to Field Place about the time that Shelley would have written the poems; but it was Elizabeth Shelley, and not Harriet Grove, who was his coadjutor in this volume. The work, however, had a brief existence, for Shelley having discovered incorporated in it a poem now supposed to have been written by "Monk" Lewis, he ordered the whole edition to be destroyed. One other literary venture with which Shelley was connected must be mentioned, viz., the *Posthumous Fragments of Margaret Nicholson.* This book had a singular origin. Shelley intimated to his friend Hogg his intention of publishing some poems anonymously, when the latter, having read them, expressed an adverse opinion upon them, though he thought they might easily be rendered into burlesque poetry. Shelley accordingly set to work and increased the amusing element in the poems, and Hogg suggested the title. Margaret Nicholson was a mad washerwoman, who had attempted the life of George III., and was incarcerated in a lunatic asylum. The volume, being uncommon in style, had considerable success in the University of Oxford. The most revolutionary sentiments were expressed, and as there was a good deal of wild talk about freedom just then, it was apparently not suspected that the work was written as burlesque, and certainly not that its authors were in such close proximity to the heads of Colleges.

But these effusions are not of substantial moment in the development of Shelley's genius, and their publication was speedily followed by sterner events. By this time every person who has read of Shelley's residence at Oxford and expulsion from the University, has formed his own definite conclusions thereupon. Yet, in what has been written, justice is frequently denied, first to the poet, and then to the authorities. As this residence of six months at Oxford, and its unhappy termination, formed one of the principal turning points in Shelley's career, it will be of importance to look at the matter somewhat closely. I must express my conviction, however, in the outset, that so great had been the progress which Shelley had made in free thought, that he would himself, at no distant date, have felt it his duty to leave the University, as a place which had become totally incompatible with his views. It must eventually have come to that, for he could never have smothered his convictions. There were more stages to pass than the authorities (had they been never so solicitous) could have aided the poet to traverse. As the matter stands, there is scarcely room for doubt that the authorities of the University behaved with great harshness to the erring student and his friend. The explanation given by Hogg of the production of the pamphlet on *The Necessity of Atheism* clearly shows, I think, that its author's judges transgressed on the side of over-severity. The whole thing was unfortunate in this respect, that while on the one hand here was an impulsive young student who could ill brook the indignity to which he was subjected, as he believed, at the

hands of the authorities—there were these authorities themselves, on the other hand, who were astounded at the daring of the youth who defied
them. At this time the very indefinite views of
Shelley upon the question of the government of
the world and the existence of God began to assume
form and substance; but I am inclined to think,
after a study of this period, that he was only
feeling for the light. He meant his pamphlet
to be as much of a tentative character as of a
declaratory one; and he would have rejoiced had
the men of accredited erudition been able to dissi-
pate the clouds of scepticism in which he was
fast becoming involved. Lady Shelley's account
of the pamphlet (and her testimony is supported
by Mr. Hogg) is as follows: " Notwithstanding the
extremely spiritual and romantic character of his
(Shelley's) genius, he applied himself to logic with
ardour and success, and of course brought it to
bear on all subjects, including theology. With
his habitual disregard of consequences, he hastily
wrote a pamphlet, in which the defective logic of
the usual arguments in favour of the existence of
a God was set forth: this he circulated among the
authorities and members of his college. In point
of fact, the pamphlet did not contain any positive
assertion; it was merely a challenge to discussion,

beginning with certain axioms, and finishing with
a Q. E. D. The publication (consisting of only
two pages) seemed rather to imply, on the part of
the writer, a desire to obtain better reasoning on
the side of the commonly received opinion, than
any wish to overthrow with sudden violence the
·grounds of men's belief. In any case, however,
had the heads of the college been men of candid
and broad intellects, they would have recognised
in the author of the obnoxious pamphlet an earnest
love of truth, a noble passion for arriving at the
nature of things, however painful the road. They
might at least have sought, by argument and
remonstrance, to set him in what they conceived
to be the right path; but either they had not the
courage and the regard for truth necessary for
such a course, or they were themselves the victims
of a narrow education. At any rate, for this
exercise of scholastic ingenuity, Shelley was
expelled." In all probability, the authorities were
not at home in discussing the troublesome questions
raised by the disputatious student. They had one
effective weapon within their grasp, however, which
they used, viz., expulsion. While not denying the
authority upon which they acted, yet which they
also somewhat strained, their general obstinacy
and density of intellect call to mind the say-

ing of Sydney Smith, when he complained that
we should never get a wooden pavement to St.
Paul's till certain ecclesiastical dignitaries " could
be persuaded to lay their heads together." From
Shelley's recorded account of the expulsion it will
be perceived that in the demeanour of the Master
there was much of the *fortiter in re*, but very little
of the *suaviter in modo*; and the best proof we
could desire that Shelley did not exaggerate in his
narration is the conduct of his friend Hogg. So
convinced was he of the gross injustice perpetrated
towards Shelley, that he endeavoured to procure a
reversal of the sentence from the authorities, but
only to share the same fate himself. With regard
to the whole subject, though I incline most nearly
to Lady Shelley's view of it, I cannot go the whole
length of her statement. She says that the poet
was expelled from Oxford, with great injustice,
" for a pamphlet which, if it had been given as a
translation of the work of some old Greek, would
have been regarded as a model of subtle metaphysical reasoning." Perhaps so; but however
admirable as a metaphysical exercise, the authorities would have been compelled to controvert its
positions. The ablest " old Greek " who ever lived
would have been dismissed from Oxford, equally
with Shelley, if he had developed and promulgated

doctrines thoroughly incompatible with the religious basis of the Colleges.   On the other hand,
De Quincey is wrong in his palliation of Shelley's
conduct when he puts it on the ground of his
extreme youth.   He asserts that at this period he
had only entered upon his sixteenth year, whereas
he had entered upon his nineteenth.   The course
which humanity should have dictated in the
matter of the pamphlet would have been to allow
some time for reflection on Shelley's part, in order
to ascertain whether he had affirmed and maintained what were real fixed principles with him ;
and in case he answered in the affirmative, then
to give him the option of withdrawal, after pointing out to him that by the very nature of his
tenets he was precluded from remaining a student
at the University.   Had this been done, the
University would have been vindicated, whilst
the heart of Shelley might have been saved one
pang, and his life one indignity—both of which
must be regarded as unquestionably severe.

The results of the expulsion were disastrous to
the poet in many ways.   Besides the anguish
which the act itself caused his sensitive spirit, his
father, not in the least understanding the disposition
of his gifted son, informed him that he could no
longer visit at Field Place except upon certain con-

ditions, to which Shelley found it impossible to accede. The bluff country member, in writing to the elder Mr. Hogg, expressed the hope that they would respectively be able to convert their sons from the error of their ways. "Paley's 'Natural Theology,' I shall recommend my young man to read," said Mr. Shelley. But his "young man" was too far gone for Paley, and remained refractory. After his dismissal from College, the intimacy between Shelley and his early love also abruptly ceased—another shaft of pain from which he suffered. Miss Grove was removed from his influence: and his correspondence with Miss Felicia Browne (afterwards Mrs. Hemans) also terminated in consequence of his heretical opinions.

. In loneliness of heart, but with the pride of his lofty mind unsubdued by the bolts of misfortune which had fallen upon him, we next behold the outcast in London. He is now almost in pecuniary embarrassment, yet the generosity of his nature is not one whit impaired; and it is affirmed that on one occasion he actually pawned his favourite solar microscope to relieve a case of distress. Shelley took lodgings in Poland Street, a locality which is said to have reminded him of Thaddeus of Warsaw and freedom; and he appears to have nearly arrived at the same straits as that favourite hero. But although his father treated him harshly, his sisters, whom he seems to have ever deeply loved, played the part of good Samaritans, sending him from their store of accumulated pocket-money sufficient to keep him from starvation. The next important incident in his life is one that, with his soul and temperament, might easily have been predicated. He fell in love. I ought, perhaps, rather to have said he was fascinated by the æsthetic appearance of the being who stirred in him this new feeling of admiration; for it would appear from subsequent events that love was too strong and too sacred a name to employ in describing the passion of Shelley for Harriet Westbrook. Certainly there was not the strength and intensity of feeling in it which he afterwards experienced for Mary Godwin. Miss Westbrook is described as a beautiful girl " with a complexion brilliant in pink and white, with hair quite like a poet's dream, and Bysshe's peculiar admiration"—that is, of a light brown colour. She was of delicate build, and at the time Shelley first saw her was about sixteen years of age. Her father was a retired hotel-keeper, and well to do. Harriet had a sister named Eliza, who was a constant butt for Mr. Hogg's ridicule, and who does not appear to have been particularly prepossessing. She had dark eyes, dark and plentiful hair, was pitted with the small-pox, had a slight figure and a Jewish aspect. Much of the unhappiness of Shelley's life for the next few years was due to the influence of this sister, as will probably be one day proven. The letters of Shelley to Hogg at and near the time of the meeting of the former with Miss Westbrook show that he had lost all hope of ever being united to Miss Grove, and possibly also his affection for her was on the wane. That he had felt keenly the disappointment in regard to her, nevertheless, is not dubious. Miss Westbrook's parents living in London, Shelley was on one occasion (after a slight indisposition from which she had suffered) chosen to escort Harriet back to school at Clapham—the same school in which were Shelley's sisters. Just at this time Sir Timothy Shelley made an amicable arrangement with his son, who found himself on a brief visit to Field Place. A new settlement of the property being arrived at, Sir Timothy agreed to make Shelley an allowance of £200 a year, and also gave him permission to live where he pleased. This latter piece of condescension was not much of a boon, seeing that the son had a will of his own ; but the money was the substantial lifting of a cloud. A short period only elapsed after this settlement when Shelley, being in North Wales on a visit to Mr. Thomas Grove, his cousin, re-

ceived an urgent summons from the sisters Westbrook to return to London. When this letter
came to Shelley, calling him back to town, he said—

> " Hear it not, Percy, for it is a knell
> That summons thee to Heaven or to Hell."

On reaching London, he found that Harriet was in
the midst of a violent quarrel with her father, who
wished to force her to return to school against her
will. Shelley took her part, and as a solution of
the difficulty Harriet was in, they eloped together
and were married in Edinburgh. ·In a letter
written to Hogg (but whose authenticity Lady
Shelley does not guarantee, though I do not see
why she should not do so) Shelley says: "I shall
certainly come to York, but Harriet Westbrook
will decide whether now or in three weeks. Her
father has persecuted her in a most horrible way
by endeavouring to compel her to go to school.
She asked my advice .. I advised her to resist.
She wrote to say that resistance was useless, but
that she would fly with me, and threw herself
upon my protection." Mr. Rossetti believes from
this that Miss Westbrook was quite ready to live
with Shelley without the ceremony of marriage:
this conjecture, however, may be harsh and unjust
towards Miss Westbrook; for it is possible that there

was some understanding of marriage implied when
Harriet expressed herself willing to elope. This
idea is further strengthened by another passage in
this same letter to Hogg, where Shelley says, "I
will hear your arguments for matrimonialism, by
which I am now almost convinced." One thing is
sufficiently clear, nevertheless—that the advances
as to the elopement were made by Miss Westbrook, though possibly with an understanding of
marriage. Yet Shelley's conduct was undoubtedly
noble at this time; for although he held peculiar
views on marriage, out of regard for Miss Westbrook, he became united with her in matrimony.
Here we arrive at what was undoubtedly one of
the most unhappy passages in his life. It could
not be expected that a man with so fine a mental
organisation, and such cravings after knowledge
and intellectual excellence, could long be satisfied
with the restricted mind which he had now made
his own. But after all exordiums upon the folly
of the transaction, the character of Shelley stands
out in regard to this marriage in excellent relief;
and no other refutation was needed of the charge
that he was a contemner of morals.

After a short residence in Edinburgh, Shelley
and his wife went to York, where they were joined
by the elder Miss Westbrook, "a visitor," says Lady

Shelley, " whose presence was in many respects unfortunate. From strength of character and disparity of years (for she was much older than Harriet), she exercised a strong influence over her sister ; and this influence was used without much discretion, and with little inclination to smooth the difficulties or promote the happiness of the young couple, whose united ages amounted to thirty-five years." This exceedingly strong-minded person appears soon to have made herself a terror both to Shelley and his wife, reducing the latter to a condition of nervousness that boded ill for her future health. She seems to have considered that she had a heaven-born mission to take charge of the poet and Mrs. Shelley, and very early in the course of his married life she had driven Shelley to the extremity of declaring that either he or she should leave the house. This fact is of some importance in view of what ultimately occurred, and shows that the ground of Shelley's dissatisfaction with his matrimonial state was partly prepared for him by this meddlesome individual, and that much of the blame for the ruined happiness of husband and wife should accrue to her. The singular anecdote is related that on one occasion, when the little party were out on an excursion in York, Harriet coolly propounded these questions to Hogg, "What is your opinion of suicide? Did you ever think of destroying yourself?" The biographer adds that she often discoursed of her purpose of killing herself some day or other; and this at great length, in a calm and resolute manner. Without building too much upon these incidents, many who have busily concerned themselves with the marriage of Shelley to Harriet Westbrook, and with its tragic ending, have failed to give due weight to untoward circumstances—due to the officious intermeddling of his wife's sister—in their eagerness to fix upon Shelley the greater portion of the blame for subsequent events. Instead of talking about the "mad Shelley," it would have been much nearer the truth to assert that it was his poor wife who was afflicted with a monomania—that of self-destruction—superinduced, no doubt, by extraneous influences. There exists abundant evidence to prove that Harriet was reduced to a state of complete wretchedness by the unwelcome presence of her sister in her new abode, and the idea of suicide was a topic she invariably discussed with the utmost freedom and fearlessness. Her life was embittered by her relative; besides which she was conscious of a hopeless and ever-widening breach between herself and her husband.

This brief statement of certain biographical facts in Shelley's life I have deemed it incumbent upon me to make, inasmuch as they played a conspicuous part in the education of the man and of the poet. It is impossible to read many of his fervid lyrics, and those highly-strung passages in the more important dramas and poems he subsequently wrote, without perceiving that they owed much of their most striking thought to his personal experience. As clearly as Byron depicted in his verse the suffering and delight of his own soul, so manifestly did Shelley draw upon his own anguish and the exaltation which proceeded from his exquisite sensibilities. Has not the author of *Julian and Maddalo* indeed himself declared that

> " Most wretched men
> Are cradled into poetry by wrong:
> They learn in suffering what they teach in song ? "

For this reason we are bound to trace the connection between his individual life and song. Save for those passages in Shelley's career, and others which it may yet be necessary to mention, who knows but that the whole tenor of his life's work might have been changed ? We have received as a heritage the poetry of inspired passion; poetry which is the outcome of obloquy, of a burning sense

of injustice, of the love of divine beauty, of deep
and fierce affection, and of an inextinguishable
devotion to humanity.

Shelley's acquaintance with Southey appears to
have had no influence in directing the genius of
the former. For some of Southey's poems he had
a high admiration, but it is scarcely possible to
conceive of a long friendship between the two.
Shelley must necessarily, sooner or later, have gone
off at a tangent. Yet, though there was very little
in common between them, they appear to have kept
for a brief period on amicable relations, if indeed
they did not cherish a close intimacy. Shelley
on one occasion evidently said something to the
elder poet respecting his married infelicity, or
Southey had discovered it for himself, for we find
the latter observing, in language which showed
that he knew how to accommodate himself to
circumstances, " A man ought to be able to live
with any woman; you see that I can, and so
ought you. It comes to pretty much the same
thing, I apprehend. There is no great choice or
difference." Southey might not have been absolutely serious in this remark upon his marital relations, and indeed most probably was not, yet his
life, like one of his best-known works, was only
one long " Commonplace Book." His books were in

reality dearer to him than the human species; but with Shelley the case was the reverse. He had a great capacity for being either intensely happy or intensely miserable; and his feelings were irresistibly enlisted in one direction or the other by those into whose society he was constantly thrown. It is imperative to remember this in endeavouring to pass judgment upon him for his share in the impending tragedy after his marriage with Harriet Westbrook. His temperament was so keen and ardent that he could not regard with indifference any associations in which he stood towards mankind.

With respect to Shelley's first marriage, it would be well if the curtain could for ever fall upon that unhappy tragedy. As that is impossible, however, it is necessary to state—holding the scales, as far as we can, with an even balance—that Shelley cannot be exonerated from blame—not for absolute harshness or wrong, but for the thoughtlessness which first led him into this marriage, and the indifference which afterwards crept over him with regard to his wife. He felt, nevertheless, that their natures were incompatible, and it was impossible for him to play the hypocrite. One thing will certainly be hereafter established, viz., that he was not responsible for his wife's death. Though the ill-assorted

union wrought both the poet and his wife much
misery, I see in this man no trace of the feeling
which would cause others to suffer, but instead
sadness and regret for pain that he might at any
time have thoughtlessly caused : even more than
that—for pain which the world would have entirely absolved him from causing, but responsi-
bility for which he was ever too ready to take
upon himself.

It has been demonstrated to a certainty that before Shelley parted from his first wife he had been
convinced of their mutual incompatibility, and
that they had lived unhappily for a considerable
period preceding the actual separation. Some
have nevertheless asserted that there was no
estrangement, and no shadow of a thought of
separation till Shelley became acquainted with
Mary Godwin. Happily for Shelley, this charge
can be disposed of. There was unquestionably a
deep estrangement; and it is just possible that
the poet might have turned to the love of Mary
Godwin as a solace in his misery; but his affection for Mary Godwin was certainly not the
origin of the unhappy condition of things between
himself and his wife. The poet only saw Mary
Godwin once till some date between April and
June 1814, whilst Shelley's own statements, and

the letters of his friends, prove that there was an estrangement between him and his wife before the latter period. The first occasion on which Shelley saw Mary Godwin was in London, in the year 1812; but the poet regarded her then as a mere child, and she made scarcely any impression upon him whatever. The whole subject-matter of contention as regards this marriage resolves itself, after an examination of authoritative documents, into these simple statements,—viz., that the separation could not have come with surprise upon Mrs. Shelley—she must have expected it would occur at some time or other; though, when Shelley left her, it is true there was no reason on her part for anticipating that he would not return, neither was there a fixed intention, *at that time*, on his part, of not returning: that the wife, equally with the husband, had become convinced they were ill-suited to each other, and that it would have been better had they never met; and, lastly, whatever may have been the precipitating causes, that the separation was the result of circumstances known to both. But just as Shelley's first elopement with Harriet Westbrook was fostered and mainly brought about by her elder sister for her own purposes, so the second elopement was greatly encouraged by Miss Clairmont, whose name is preserved in connection with

Byron, and who ought to have known better—while at this time Mary Godwin was only a girl of sixteen. The world knows the disastrous end of Mrs. Shelley; but upon whom shall be placed the blame of that tragedy? He would be a bold man who undertook thoroughly to solve that now insoluble problem. We know, however, that Shelley—as, indeed, might be readily imagined—was deeply affected by the event. Leigh Hunt declares that it completely unmanned him for a period, and that he suffered remorse at having brought his wife into a sphere which she was not qualified to fill. One writer says—" I am well aware that he had suffered severely, and that he continued to be haunted by certain recollections, partly real and partly imaginative, which pursued him like an Orestes." Captain Medwin affirmed that the sad circumstance ever after threw a cloud over the poet, and all biographers speak of the genuineness and strength of his sorrow. It may be assumed as indisputable, however, that Mrs. Shelley's death had no direct and immediate relation to the differences between herself and her husband. The fact that Shelley once proclaimed himself an Atheist has been quite sufficient in the eyes of many to prove that he was capable of conduct directly leading to

the death of his wife, or, indeed, that he was
equal to the commission of almost any other
enormity.   It is always your "hard-and-fast-line"
Christian who is severest in his censures upon
humanity—that being who clings tenaciously to
the letter, but exhibits very little of the spirit of
Christianity.   It was doubtless some such knowledge as this that Shelley possessed of his traducers
which led him to breathe open defiance to the
world, and which has given to us one of the most
tragic exhibitions of man fighting against fate to
be found in the annals of mankind.

Carlyle speaks of Shelley "filling the earth with
inarticulate wail; like the infinite, inarticulate
grief and weeping of forsaken infants."   In some
respects this is a brief but accurate digest of the
poet's life; in others, it bears in it small remnant
of appropriateness.   In that Shelley was driven to
wild despair by the injustice of the world, which
led him to send up such a wail to heaven as hath
rarely been heard from the voice of gifted mortal
such as he, Carlyle's definition is good: if it be
meant to represent Shelley's accomplished work, it
is wholly inadequate in expression.   It is true
that, as we have seen, he was "cradled into poetry
by wrong," and some notes of his divine music
have been marred in consequence.   Naturally, his

voice should not have been given to wailing; he
was fitted to be one of the most competent utterers
and interpreters of the great harmonies of the universe. His apprehensions of beauty and of the
Divinity should have been clearer than those of
most other mortals; now and then there is a shaft
of light in his poetry which seems to pierce
even away into the Infinite; but the darkness of
desolation fell upon him, and he was outraged and
blinded by grief and anger because he could not
find the Christian's God in the Christian.

No rhapsody, or misinterpretation of the issues
of this man's life, will this affirmation be found to
appear when it is grasped in its full significance.
On the very threshold of existence Shelley was
thrown from the natural track of his spirit, and he
found himself, even in boyhood, in an antagonism
with the world, deeper and more complete than
often falls to riper manhood. The jar thus caused
was never overset. It was not a great mind un-
hinged, as some have vainly supposed; it was a
great heart driven from its moorings and unable in
the long subsequent years to find anchor. The
wonder should be, not that one of his temperament occasionally railed at society, but that he
should have preserved his noble aspirations and
volitions through all this.

Two events in his life I have just dealt with because of a belief that they were great operating causes in the production of much which we discover in Shelley's writings. To what, for instance, do we owe *Queen Mab*, a poem which, for some inscrutable reason or another, is frequently associated with the name of Shelley, as though it were at once both the flower and fruit of his genius? It was simply the crying out of a sensitive spirit against that by which it had been injured and crushed. It took the wild form of rank infidelity from a strong feeling of disgust which animated the writer, at the time of its production, against those professors of religion whose lives were all that the young poet had to argue upon in search of the truth or the falsity of their doctrines. The poem is the autobiography of Shelley in his youth, and when the mind was in a transition state. What does he himself say upon the subject? Some years after its publication he writes :—" I doubt not but that it is perfectly worthless in point of literary composition; and that, in all that concerns moral and political speculation, as well as in the subtler discriminations of metaphysical and religious doctrine, it is still more crude and immature. I am a devoted enemy to religious, political, and domestic oppression; and I regret this publication, not so much from literary vanity as because I fear it is better fitted to injure than to serve the sacred cause of freedom." Further on in the same letter he has these significant observations—" Whilst I exonerate myself from all share in having divulged opinions hostile to exist- ing sanctions, under the form, whatever it may be, which they assume, in this poem, it is scarcely necessary for me to protest against the system of inculcating the truth of Christianity or the excel- lence of monarchy, however true or however excel- ent they may be, by such equivocal arguments as confiscation and imprisonment, and invective and slander, and the insolent violation of the most sacred ties of nature and society." After these ex- pressions, and other proofs which could be adduced to the same effect, it is not a little singular to find it calmly assumed that *Queen Mab* is the full ex- pression of its author's beliefs, or rather nega- tion of beliefs, respecting religion and God—a position from which he never swerved. Nothing could be more unjust than such an assumption, in view of the overwhelming evidence existing to the contrary.

I shall not be the apologist for unquestionable errors which Shelley committed; that would be to believe him already in possession of the perfection of humanity for which he strove: neither on the

other hand will I be a silent witness when any
stone is ruthlessly cast at his memory.   It is impossible, for instance, to apportion the precise
blame which should fall to his lot in connection
with the circumstances of his first marriage and its
results ; but it may unhesitatingly be said, and with
perfect accuracy and truth, that he has been much
maligned in this matter.   Even so fine and genial a
spirit as James Russell Lowell has adopted some of
the charges as genuine from which it was to be hoped
Shelley had been cleared, and he takes too gross a
view of the relations between Shelley and Mary
Godwin.   Mr. Lowell has doubtless erred through
defective information ; but in other cases this is
not so.   How strange it is that man should be so
much more on the alert to mark the evil rather
than the good in his fellow-man !   Of all lives of
great men with which the world is acquainted, this
has been most peculiarly the case with Shelley.
Transcendent as were his virtues when compared
with his faults, the lime-light of a malevolent
scrutiny has been turned on the latter, while the
former have rarely, if ever, been brought into the
prominence they deserve.   If to be an apologist
for Shelley is to endeavour to show the man truly
as he was, then I would rank with his apologists,
ardently longing that the ability of the defence

were more commensurate with the strength of its inspiration.

Let me admit at once, however, in arriving at a consideration of another important event in Shelley's life—his elopement with Mary Godwin —that the poet's conduct cannot be defended. He set at naught the customs of society. The fact that, by the teachings of her father and the writings of her mother, the mind of Miss Godwin had become familiarised with the idea that marriage was one of those institutions which a nobler era of mankind would inevitably sweep away, did not relieve Shelley and his companion from their obligations to society as constituted. That new era not having arrived, it is obvious that to resolve at once to be governed by its laws was a foolish act, and one not tending to the well-being of society. There is a certain grandeur in the dream that the world will one day be a great commonwealth, in which men will share and share alike; but it would be both inconvenient and objectionable if my neighbour endeavoured forcibly to bring about this equalisation by making a raid upon my property. We cannot yet get rid of the policeman in morals. But having said this, our condemnation of Shelley refines into pity and sympathy when we remember him as he actually appeared on his second meeting with Mary Godwin. By reason of his very nature he was sorrowing with no light sorrow, and was afflicted with no common melancholy. There is something touching in the story as related by Lady Shelley :—"It was in the society and sympathy of the Godwins that Shelley sought and found some relief in his present sorrow. He was still extremely young. His anguish, his isolation, his difference from other men, his gifts of genius, and eloquent enthusiasm, made a deep impression on Godwin's daughter Mary, now a girl of sixteen, who had been accustomed to hear Shelley spoken of as something rare and strange. To her, as they met one eventful day in St. Pancras churchyard, by her mother's grave, Bysshe in burning words poured forth the tale of his wild past—how he had suffered, how he had been misled, and how, if supported by her love, he hoped in future years to enrol his name with the wise and good who had done battle for their fellow-men, and been true through all adverse storms to the cause of humanity. Unhesitatingly she placed her hand in his, and linked her fortune with his own." And a beautiful union of souls this after-wards proved, for love and reverence were never more strongly blended or apparent than in the passion which was only severed in these hearts by

death.   Indefensible as the act of elopement was
in the eyes of society, I believe that Shelley's love
for Mary Godwin was the only thing that saved
him when a greater trouble than almost any which
he had yet endured overtook him.

Shelley's friendship with the philosopher William Godwin is one of the most interesting passages of literary history.   It began in romance,
and culminated in genuine affection.   The author
of *Political Justice* came of a Nonconformist
family, and, having been educated at the Hoxton
College, was himself for some time a Nonconformist
minister.   The close spirit of speculation, however,
in which he indulged, led to a change in his
religious opinions, and, resigning his ministerial
position, he devoted himself still more assiduously
to historical and metaphysical inquiries.   His novel
of *Caleb Williams* is distinguished for an originality
which entirely removes it from the category of
ordinary fiction.   The man himself is a striking
figure, from his noble independence of character, and
the absence of personal feeling which marked the
whole course of his polemical strife.   He succeeded
in attracting as his disciples some of the best spirits
of the age, by whom the philosopher was regarded
with mingled feelings of affection and veneration.
Shelley, inflamed with the desire to be of some

use to his species, was not likely to remain unknown to Godwin for any length of time. Accordingly, in the year 1812, and while residing at
Keswick with his young wife, he wrote a letter to
Godwin, in which is to be distinctly traced a fine
spirit of enthusiasm, yet one, for want of proper
direction, which threatened to be of no advantage
to society. In the course of his communication the
writer observes :—" I have but just entered on the
scene of human operations; yet my feelings and
my reasonings correspond with what yours were.
My course has been short, but eventful. I have
seen much of human prejudice, suffered much from
human persecution, yet I see no reason hence
inferrible which should alter my wishes for their
renovation. The ill-treatment I have met with has
more than ever impressed the truth of my principles
on my judgment. I am young. I am ardent in
the cause of philanthropy and truth; do not suppose
that this is vanity; I am not conscious that it influences this portraiture. I imagine myself dis-
passionately describing the state of my mind. I
am young. You have gone before me,—I doubt
not, are a veteran to me in the years of persecution.
Is it strange that, defying prejudice, as I have done,
I should outstep the limits of custom's prescription,
and endeavour to make my desire useful by a

E

friendship with William Godwin ?"   Godwin does
not quite seem to have known what to make of this
letter from a Paladin who was anxious to "ride
abroad redressing human wrongs;" but he afterwards took kindly to Shelley; and the latter, in
another epistle to the philosopher, confesses to being
filled with the most intoxicating sensations that
Godwin should have been brought to feel a deep
and earnest interest in his welfare.   The specific
public results which sprang from their friendship
cannot be dwelt upon at this juncture, but one
thought it is difficult to repress, viz., the singularity
of the fact that two men differing so utterly in their
mental organisation should have been brought into
close union.   On the occasion of Shelley's visit to
Ireland, he discovered the full value of the philosopher's superior wisdom ; and if the poet at more
than one subsequent period was rebellious under
Godwin's advice, there never was an instance when,
as quickly as he discovered it, he did not frankly
confess his error.   In one juncture Shelley sought
Godwin's aid and judgment upon literary matters,
and the letter he received in reply is a remarkable
specimen both of sound judgment and criticism.
After referring to the proper attitude of the student
in considering the life's work of great men, he
proceeds to say :—" Shakspeare, Bacon, and Milton

are the three greatest contemplative characters that this island has produced. As I put Shakspeare and Milton at the head of our poetry, I put Bacon and Milton at the head of our prose. Yet what astonishing prose writers had we in Sir Thomas Browne and Jeremy Taylor! not to mention two others, only inferior to them, Robert Burton and Izaak Walton. Hobbes and Shelton also, as prose translators, may almost rank with Chapman in verse." He then compares these writers with the more modern, concluding by a pungent personal application:—"Those were the times when authors thought. Every line is pregnant with sense, and the reader is inevitably put to the expense of thinking likewise. The writers were richly furnished with conception, imagination, and feeling; and out of the abundance of their hearts flowed the lucubrations they committed to paper. *You* have what appears to me a false taste in poetry. You love a perpetual sparkle and glittering, such as are to be found in Darwin, and Southey, and Scott, and Campbell." Putting out of court all questions upon theological matters, there were just those qualities of robustness of intellect and firmness of purpose in Godwin which were invaluable to the poet at this period, when he was in danger of allowing his prodigious talents to become mere wasted forces. One result of the correspondence which passed between the poet and the philosopher was that Shelley set himself to the study of history, which he described as a "record of crimes and miseries." Of the total sum of Godwin's influence over the young student we have no adequate conception; but while the intimacy confirmed Shelley in proving all things, to see whether they were honest and true, fearless as to the consequences of inquiry, it doubtless also led him into a more exact mode of thinking and writing—which indeed is observable in his poems after he had sat at the feet of this philosophical Gamaliel. And Godwin was admirably seconded by his daughter. In her love and counsel Shelley at length discovered his sheet anchor. To her he could unburthen himself, not only looking confidently for sympathy, but also for intellectual appreciation and interchange of ideas. An apparent insolence in the expression of his infidelity now gave place to moderation, though the extreme nature of his views was unflinchingly shared by his wife. Shelley's second love, who was five years his junior, is described as "rather short, remarkably fair, and light-haired, with brownish grey eyes, a great forehead, striking features, and a noticeable air of sedateness." One writer has compared her to the classic bust of Clytie. Careless

as to her personal appearance, she exhibited qualities of mind which fully challenged Shelley's
admiration; she had received by nature a large
share of the endowments of her parents. The
strength of her character, and the acuteness of her
intellect, made her an inestimable companion for
her erratic husband, whose love for her appears to
have amounted almost to idolatry. Of her feelings
towards him, some idea may be gathered from the
passionate bursts of anguish written in her diary
after his melancholy death.

More bitter than almost any experience through
which Shelley was called upon to pass—making
the already impassable gulf between him and
society still deeper and wider—was that which
arose out of the Chancery suit in regard to his
children. Shelley desiring to have possession of
his offspring after his first wife's death, Mr. Westbrook refused to give them up, and instituted proceedings in Chancery, filing a bill in which he
alleged that their father was unfit to have charge
of them on account of the alleged depravity of his
religious and moral opinions. It is more than
possible that this was not the real motive for Mr.
Westbrook's proceedings, but rather that in consequence of what had gone before, and remembering
his daughter's miserable fate, he had determined

to thwart Shelley in this important matter.
Whether such a speculation be correct or not,
however, history records the decree that Shelley
was not allowed to have the custody of his own
children. Yet, though the poet's character was
ruled to be dangerous, and offensive to public
morals, the poet's pocket was drawn upon in order
to pay for teachings in which he did not believe.
For this purpose he was mulcted in a sum of £200
a year. Widely as I differ from Shelley's religious
opinions, there is that in this decree of Lord Eldon's
which strikes a severe blow at the strict principles
of justice. Justice, in fact, was defeated on that
very judgment seat where it is supposed to be
enshrined. Let us see to what dilemma the support of such a decree would lead. It gives the
power into the hands of the Lord Chancellor of
saying what opinions should and should not be
taught to a child, and makes him more the absolute
master of human souls than the parents of the
children whose cases are decided before him. Lord
Eldon did not define precisely where the line was
to be drawn in sceptical opinions, beyond which,
if a man passed, he was to be branded as totally
unfit to retain the possession of his children. By
what right was the Lord Chancellor's orthodoxy
to overrule Shelley's unorthodoxy? According to

his decision, it would seem that the surviving maternal relatives of any child might procure its custody from the father, if they held ordinary religious views, and that father professed, let us say, Moravian or Sandemanian principles. It is impossible to agree with those who say that Shelley had no ground for complaint in being deprived of his children. The outraged heart of the father is the best answer to that, whilst the harshness of the decree was made still more apparent from the fact that Shelley had nominated as guardian of his children (if yielded up to him) a lady who was in every respect qualified to fulfil the charge. This bitter trouble probably sank deeper into Shelley's soul than any other. He has repeated references to it, which mark the keenness of his anguish—an anguish which time failed to obliterate. One terrible poem he wrote upon the author of his woe and despair, and in his *Masque of Anarchy* he further described the Lord Chancellor in these scathing lines :—

> " Next came Fraud, and he had on,
> Like Lord Eldon, an ermine gown ;
> His big tears (for he wept well)
> Turn'd to mill-stones as they fell :
>
> " And the little children, who
> Round his feet play'd to and fro,
> Thinking every tear a gem,
> Had their brains knock'd out by them."

The spectacle of a divinely-gifted man, thus buffeted to and fro, with the measure of his sorrows proportioned apparently by fate, in subtle irony, to the greatness of his capacity for suffering, is one which would surely move any human being to pity. Circumstances appeared always to fight against Shelley; his sensitive nature was continually subjected to trials from which more phlegmatic spirits are exempt. Restless and agitated as the sea, the billows were ever surging round his heart, and never falling into peace and calm. Some of those incidents in his life which have begotten the numerous passages of fiery indignation and invective in his poems have been already glanced at. The misery which he caused to others bore no proportion to the misery which fell upon himself. And yet, when the dross of his nature has been weighed to the uttermost grain, it is contemptible and insignificant compared with the genuine gold of which he was mostly wrought. I have reviewed the preparation which Shelley had in the school of adversity for the work to which all his suffering was but the introduction. And in this lies the key to the development of his character. From the unfortunate and the unhappy, we cannot fail to educe further and almost unique interest when we pass to another phase of his existence, and see how this being, who was the sport of destiny, endeavoured to lift humanity—by the spirit of sacrifice—to that height of dignity and happiness which had been the dream and ambition of his life. Shelley, as we shall now behold him, is but the natural sequence to the Shelley already foreshadowed and prefigured.

II.

POLITICIAN, ATHEIST, PHILANTHROPIST.

> " We are assured
> Much may be conquered, much may be endured,
> Of what degrades and crushes us. We know
> That we have power over ourselves to do
> And suffer—*what*, we know not till we try ;
> But something nobler than to live and die."
>
> *Julian and Maddalo.*

II.

POLITICIAN, ATHEIST, PHILANTHROPIST.

THE sublime picture presented by the Greek dramatist, of a great and heroic being struggling against
adversity and the gods, seems almost to find its
modern counterpart in Shelley. We have previously seen, and shall yet more clearly witness, how
he battled with the inequalities and miseries of the
world. That a super-sensitive poet, and one in
whom the imagination held dominant sway, should
exhibit the keenest desire to benefit his fellow-men
in numberless practical modes, is one of the most
singular episodes in literature. Yet the intensity
of Shelley's devotion to these objects was such that
if his intellectual powers had been less strong and
comprehensive, we should have been forced to the
conclusion that he was a mere enthusiast and fana-
tic. A study of the method of his life, however, on
its practical side, will lead to the opposite result,
and convince us that his schemes for the ameliora-

tion of mankind sprang from a strong heart and not
from an ill-balanced mind; that he was in reality
far in advance of the age in which he lived—it
is to be feared in advance even of ages yet to
come.   Had it not been that from the religious point
of view "that atheist Shelley" was a bugbear to
society, we should have heard more of some aspects
of his character which might justly make his name
illustrious.   Nevertheless, after a dispassionate examination and sifting of his various projects and
panaceas, and in spite of his own firm belief that
he was fitted to cope with the practical government of men, I incline to the opinion that he was
better adapted to be the purifier of existing systems
than the originator of others.   Binding up the
wounds of humanity, and pouring in the oil and
wine as the good Samaritan, gave a natural outflow
to that all-pervading sympathy which seemed to
throw a halo over his other characteristics.   His
impetuosity, and the wonderful force and direct-
ness of his moral sense, interfered probably with
that just attitude of the judgment which should
primarily distinguish the reformer who moves by
gradual stages—one who does not proceed to legislative action until he has carefully weighed all
objections, and obtained a satisfactory basis which
permits of no injustice to one man while a benefit

is being secured for his brother. Impatience is fatal to organic changes in society, and however beautiful may be the enthusiasm which glows in the earnest reformer, if it be not supported by other convincing and concrete qualities, it is apt to be evanescent and to fail in accomplishing its end. Now, Shelley was rather a destroyer than a builder; his eye was intently fixed upon one object; he desired to break up utterly the wrong and corruption of the world. As to the processes by which this grand result was to be achieved, he was not always clear; albeit he never wavered in carrying on the war against error and superstition. His enthusiasm was as noble and disinterested as that of any other man whose history has been bequeathed to us; and it extorted even from Byron the remark that Shelley was the best as well as the ablest man he had ever known. It was in consequence of the persecution which the author of *Queen Mab* suffered, that Byron also affirmed his belief that if the Christ people professed to worship reappeared in the flesh they would again crucify him. So that we have not to deal with a man who found a reciprocating sympathy in others, but with one who, in spite of the great excellence of his personal character and his benevolent purposes towards mankind, was hated with a malignity which was as singular and wicked as it was profoundly mysterious.

That was a drastic political programme with which Shelley, who had only just passed his nineteenth year, crossed the Channel, for the purpose of expounding it before the Irish people. Catholic Emancipation and a Repeal of the Union were the two chief points of his charter, and although at the time of his brief Irish campaign these points must to many persons have seemed the height of absurdity, Catholic Emancipation became an absolute fact a few years after the poet's death. Here, at any rate, is evidence that, to some extent, the youthful reformer read the needs of oppressed Ireland aright. Godwin overwhelmed Shelley with the most lugubrious vaticinations respecting his visit to Ireland, and said he felt it poignantly that the poet should probably have been led to take this step through reading his *Political Justice*. The philosopher added—" Shelley, you are preparing a scene of blood ! If your Associations take effect to any extensive degree, tremendous consequences will follow, and hundreds, by their calamities and premature fate, will expiate your error. And then what will it avail you to say, ' I warned them against this ; when I put the seed into the ground I laid my solemn injunctions upon it, that it should not germinate ? ' " Godwin appears to have had almost a morbid horror of associations, and his hostility to them is scarcely compatible with the exercise of that reason which peculiarly characterised him. If associations and institutions have in numbers of cases worked unmitigated evil, and do now—on the other hand, without their aid much good must remain unsecured. The perfecting and not the abolition of associations is what will ultimately prove of service to humanity. Shelley had the courage to pursue his own course, and though his visit to Ireland was abortive in one respect, yet the fact remains, as a writer has well pointed out, that "an association, the mere probability of which Godwin looked upon with terror as inevitably leading to bloodshed, anarchy, and defeat, carried its point successfully, without violence, and without even a word of insulting exultation over those who opposed it."[1] Yet in many minor details I have no doubt whatever that the philosopher's clearer general wisdom was useful in curbing the exuberance of the poet, and instrumental in controlling the fiery element of his character, which might have proved disastrous to him had it remained altogether unchecked.

Shelley was no more mistaken with regard to

[1] *Shelley's Early Life.* By Denis Florence MacCarthy.

F

Ireland than have been many eminent statesmen who, for the last fifty years, have found it a problem whose full solution is not even yet perceived. Experienced politicians would, of course, regard with derision any attempt by a mere youth to deal with a problem which had overtaxed their own energies; and the apparently chimerical nature of Shelley's project doubtless lent force to the absurd charge that the poet was afflicted with frenzy or madness. The enthusiast always has to encounter this charge from the critic, for the latter would not move in the elevation of the species unless the means he used were such as to free him from adverse comment. The enthusiast, on the contrary, goes, if necessary, with his life in his hand, as well as cherishing a very decided and wholesome contempt for obloquy. Shelley was positively in physical danger during his stay in Ireland, for at that time there existed in England one of the most miserable of all modern Governments, and his Majesty's councils were, in Irish matters, very largely swayed by an infamous man whose despicable character differentiated him from all other statesmen who ever wielded political power in this country. The treatment which the Government meted out to many of the best patriots both of this and the sister isle, was such as to make the very nation blush for its boasted progress. Treachery, that black and hideous bird, was flying hither and thither, betraying good men and true, and Shelley knew not but that his turn also to be betrayed might speedily arrive. Moreover, all his private friends were endeavouring to dissuade him from his task of recommending pacificatory measures; while Southey, for whom he had hitherto had a profound respect, had completely changed his views on the subject of Ireland and the Irish. This was a bitter blow to Shelley, and it is not matter for surprise that his admiration for his friend, in consequence of his apparent tergiversation, was speedily on the wane. Many who indulge a strong feeling of delight in the works of the author of *Thalaba*, find it impossible to deny that he laid himself open to the strictures of Byron in the dedication of *Don Juan*, when he thus closes his apostrophe :—

> " My politics as yet are all to educate :
>   Apostasy's so fashionable, too,
> To keep *one* creed's a task grown quite Herculean ;
>   Is it not so, my Tory, ultra-Julian ?"

Certainly, Southey was far from being a model of constancy in his views upon any subject; his political creed, especially, resembled that of the American candidate, who was dubious whether it coincided

with that of his auditors, yet considerately and
conveniently remarked, " Such are my views,
gentlemen; but if they don't suit, they can be
altered." At one time Southey liked the Irish,
giving them credit for the possession of genius;
but in 1811 Shelley writes in a letter—" Southey
hates the Irish; he speaks against Catholic Emancipation. In all these things we differ." But
neither Southey nor any other person could pro-
selytise Shelley from his beliefs, and he exhibited a singular tenacity of judgment as well
as strength of conviction. It is worth while to
examine briefly his *Address to the Irish People*,
of which some hundreds of copies were speedily
put into circulation. Shelley and his wife themselves distributed a great number of copies of the
pamphlet from the balcony of a house in Lower
Sackville Street. The appearance of the young
English poet on such a mission in Ireland naturally created considerable excitement amongst the
population. With regard to the pamphlet, it is very
eloquent in parts, and in some other respects has
scarcely received justice at the hands of those who
have examined it,—Godwin amongst the number,
for instance. The latter complained that Shelley,
together with all too fervent and impetuous reformers, lacked the power of perceiving that almost

every institution or form of society was good in its place, and in the period of time to which it belonged. "How many beautiful and admirable effects," says the philosopher, "grew out of Popery and the monastic institution, in the period when they were in their genuine health and vigour! To them we owe almost all our logic and our literature." But surely Shelley was not ignorant of these facts? and we cannot but think Godwin did him a little injustice in this matter. Because in the heat of argument, and for polemical purposes, Shelley made no reference to these things in his *Address*, it by no means follows that he either wilfully ignored, or was ignorant of their probability. He had one object in view, and bent his mind to the accomplishment of it, and for the time being that was all his excitable temperament allowed him to do under the circumstances. The pamphlet was not so much intended to convince by the coldness of its logic as to rouse by the breadth of its sentiment, and for the attainment of this object it was excellently devised. The author himself said in the advertisement of his pamphlet, "The lowest possible price is set on this publication, because it is the intention of the author to awaken in the minds of the Irish poor a knowledge of their real state, summarily pointing

out the evils of that state, and suggesting rational
means of remedy." The Address opens by enforcing the necessity of toleration on the part of all
religionists, and it is not sparing in its rebukes of
the Roman Catholics (the very people whom the
writer addressed) for the persecutions of which
they had been guilty in past times; certainly a
bold proceeding on the part of one wishing to convert his hearers to his own views, but one fully
showing the ingenuous nature of Shelley's mind.
The noble liberality of his sentiments is apparent
in the following passage—" Do not inquire if a
man be a heretic, if he be a Quaker, a Jew, or a
Heathen; but if he be a virtuous man, if he loves
liberty and truth, if he wish the happiness and
peace of human kind. If a man be ever so much
a believer and love not these things, he is a heart-
less hypocrite, a rascal, and a knave. Despise and
hate him as ye despise a tyrant and a villain. Oh,
Ireland! thou emerald of the ocean, whose sons
are generous and brave, whose daughters are
honourable, and frank, and fair, thou art the isle on
whose green shores I have desired to see the
standard of liberty erected—a flag of fire—a beacon
at which the world shall light the torch of Freedom!" This may have been unpleasant writing
to Lord Castlereagh, but it is not very inflam-

mable stuff in itself. Shelley next deals with the
Protestants, and after proving that they also have
been wickedly intolerant, he proceeds to demonstrate
the folly of persecuting men for their religion. He
then exhorts the Irish to disclaim violence in seeking their ends, and to trust their cause solely to its
truth. In prophetic words he foretells the triumph
of Catholic Emancipation, adding, " I do not see
that anything but violence and intolerance amongst
yourselves can leave an excuse to your enemies
for continuing your slavery." Other reforms and
blessings to humanity are to follow, as men are
purified and raised from their debasement by virtue
and knowledge. Passing on to another subject he
remarks that " the liberty of the press is placed as
a sentinel to alarm us when any attempt is made
on our liberties. It is this sentinel, oh, Irishmen,
whom I now awaken ! I create to myself a freedom
which exists not. There is no liberty of the press
for the subjects of British Government." Mr.
Finnerty, an Irishman, at that moment languished
in an English gaol for a press libel, and Shelley
had taken up his cause warmly, writing and speaking on his behalf. The Address is really a fine
rhetorical effort, but to show that Shelley did not
depend upon it as a final means for the accomplishment of his design, he appended a postscript, in

which he said—"For the purpose of obtaining the emancipation of the Catholics from the penal laws that aggrieve them, and a repeal of the Legislative Union Act, and grounding upon the remission of the church-craft and oppression, which caused these grievances, a plan of amendment and regeneration in the moral and political state of society on a comprehensive and systematic philanthropy which shall be sure though slow in its projects; and as it is without the danger and rapidity of revolution, so will it be devoid of the time-servingness of temporising reform—which in its deliberate capacity, having investigated the state of the Government of England, shall oppose those parts of it, by intellectual force, which will not bear the touchstone of reason. . . . I conclude with the words of Lafayette, a name endeared by its peerless bearer to every lover of the human race, 'For a nation to love liberty, it is sufficient that she knows it; to be free it is sufficient that she wills it.'" A few days after this Address appeared, Shelley addressed a great meeting in Fishamble Street Theatre, Dublin. It seems by the reports in the Irish papers to have been an excitable discourse, and though in one part of it, when Shelley spoke of religion, he elicited signs of disapprobation, he succeeded in favourably impressing his audience. One speaker referred to

the generous eloquence of the young Protestant
from England. The weight of evidence certainly
goes to prove that, on the whole, Shelley was very
favourably received, though—as is the case in all
public meetings of this kind—there were a few
turbulent spirits determined on breaking the peace.
An Englishman who heard Shelley on this memorable occasion, and who hated him for the views
he expressed, testified nevertheless to the power
of his oratory, and the ecstasy of the audience,
in a letter to the *Dublin Journal*. These tributes
to Shelley have only been recovered within the
last few years by the research of Mr. MacCarthy,
and this would probably account for the fact that
an opposite view had hitherto been entertained of
Shelley's visit to Ireland, a view which was also
to some extent adopted by Lady Shelley.

One is astounded at the intellectual force and
fertility which could alternate at nineteen the
production of such poems as *Queen Mab* and those
which immediately succeeded it, with the drawing
up of formal Proposals for an Association "which
shall have for its immediate objects Catholic
Emancipation and the Repeal of the Act of Union
between Great Britain and Ireland; and grounding
on the removal of these grievances an annihilation
or palliation of whatever moral or political evil it

may be within the compass of human power to
assuage or eradicate." There are frequent sentences
in these " Proposals " which are sententious, eloquent, and imbued with the spirit of a strong and
true philosophy. As a whole, they lack reason-
ableness, and to that extent Godwin's criticism of
them was accurate ; but they were unreasonable
simply because they pre-supposed that all to whom
they were addressed would at once apprehend their
spirit and forthwith endeavour to carry them into
effect. Man is a reasonable animal, it is true, but
not in the bulk ; it is the individual who does
duty for the community ; for, as we have been reminded, the fools· in every age are in a majority.
Shelley, however, lost sight of this fact, and addressed
men everywhere, and under all circumstances, as
being amenable to reason ; an error to which his
eyes were afterwards partially opened, begetting in
him thereby no small measure of disgust. It would
be curious to know what the Government of the
time thought of the poet's proposals for a monster
Association ; but the proposals themselves appear
to be drawn up with calmness and dignity. The
rhetoric is tempered, and the logic placed in
the forefront. The writer proceeds to remark
that his association would question established
principles, and though a philanthropic associa-

tion has nothing to fear from the English Constitution, which is always capable of widening
and strengthening its basis, it may expect dangers
from its government; but that fact only proved
the necessity for such an institution. And to
justify himself for thus appealing for help towards
gaining the grand end he contemplates, the author
reminds the people of Ireland that "though the
Parliament of England were to pass a thousand
bills, to inflict upon those who determined to utter
their thoughts a thousand penalties, it could not
render that criminal which was in its nature
innocent before the passing of such bills." In
these pages there is a vigorous onslaught upon
the principles of Mr. Malthus, and Shelley also
endeavours to show that the French philosophers
Voltaire, Rousseau, Helvetius, and Condorcet, were
only partial reformers of society, and consequently failed in their work of renovation. But
what of the practical effect of these eloquent proposals for a gigantic philanthropic Association?
Alas! in searching for the answer we must turn
to the disappointed Shelley, in his lodgings in Dublin, after he had cast forth his doctrines upon the
world, waiting for converts to his principles, when
no man came unto him! The revulsion of feeling
must have been great when hope was destroyed in

the bosom of this sanguine reformer, who had not
yet attained his twentieth year. Kings, Parliaments,
and society had never yet accomplished what he saw
foreshadowed to a surety in his proposals, and his
joy was turned into bitterness. Shall we laugh at
the optimist spirit which had thus gone out of itself,
and prophesied blessedness for the whole of the
human race? or shall we yield to him the sentiment of affection for the manifestation of his noble
and absorbing desires? The latter is demanded
from us, even though mental conviction of the
futile character of his schemes goes side by side
with the sentiment. Doubtless Shelley moved, or
desired to move, too fast ; and Godwin truly pricked
the bubble when he told Shelley that he exhorted
persons whom he had himself described as " of
scarcely greater elevation in the scale of intellectual
being than the oyster—thousands huddled together,
one mass of animated filth," to take the redress of
grievances into their own hands. The poet began
building the perfect edifice of humanity by laying its
topmost stone before the foundations. Although, as
we have seen, he exhibited greater political insight
than the philosopher, the latter was able ruthlessly
to shatter the various stages by which he hoped to
arrive at his end. Godwin argumentatively pleads
with his young admirer in these terms : " You say,

'What has been done within the last twenty years?'
Oh that I could place you on the pinnacle of ages,
from which these twenty years would shrink to an
invisible point! It is not after this fashion that
moral causes work in the eye of Him who looks
profoundly through the vast, and, allow me to add,
venerable machine of human society. But so
reasoned the French revolutionists. Auspicious
and admirable materials were working in the general mind of France; but these men said, as you
say, 'When we look on the last twenty years we
are seized with a sort of moral scepticism—we must
own we are eager that something should be done.'
And see what has been the result of their doings! He
that would benefit mankind on a comprehensive
scale, by changing the principles and elements of
society, must learn the hard lesson—to put off self
and to contribute by a quiet but incessant activity
like a rill of water, to irrigate and fertilise the intellectual soil." Sound but cruel advice to one
who would change the face of society in a day.
There is no disputing the accuracy of the philosopher's position. Eighteen hundred years ago
England was inhabited by savages, and even at this
day we have not completely exorcised the order,
for statistics demonstrate that there is a goodly per-
centage of the population of this Christian country

who annually kick their wives to death. Exasperating as the slow growth of benevolence and virtue may be, we cannot unduly hasten the process, and a strictly political basis of operation will never ensure the happiness of the entire race, or bathe the universe in "sweetness and light."

Knowing what is at length proved concerning Shelley's great interest in political matters, and his solicitude for the welfare of the people of the United Kingdom, we experience no difficulty in utterly discrediting the random statement of one of his biographers that he hated newspapers, and that none ever reached him while at the University. On the face of it, it is an incredible statement, and the poet's own verified correspondence places its complete inaccuracy beyond a doubt. Even while at Oxford, it is clearly shown that Shelly was " alive to the passing political events of the day, writing to the editors of newspapers, identifying himself with their opinions, congratulating them on their triumphs, indignant at their persecution, and, stranger than all, publishing a poem for the sustainment in prison of one of them who was considered by the leading Liberals of the day, as well as by Shelley, a martyr for the liberty of the Press." More than one of his biographers assert that they never saw Shelley reading a newspaper, and yet at the time of his acquaintance with them he was taking a keen interest in newspaper warfare, and writing to several journals. Even a Boswell is sometimes caught napping, but this is not surprising when we remember that *aliquando bonus Homerus dormitat.* Mr, Peacock's papers in *Fraser* show that Shelley read with great avidity the writings of Cobbett, Leigh Hunt, and others, in the political journals ; and whatever may be believed as to his fitness to cope with political problems, it is an unquestionable fact that at one time they occupied a considerable portion of his thoughts. In one letter, written in September 1819, Shelley says, " Pray let me have the earliest *political* news which you consider important at this crisis ;" and in another he says, writing from Leghorn, " Many thanks for your attention in sending the papers which contain the terrible and important news from Manchester." At the very time, in truth, during which Shelley was said to have displayed an incurable aversion to newspapers, he was considering the project of floating one himself, of which he purposed to retain the supreme direction.

Further, as a follower of Milton in declaring for the free and unfettered liberty of the press, Shelley wrote a letter to Lord Ellenborough which, as regards some of its passages, is unsurpassed in eloquence by any prose writer since the time of the sublime poet who penned the *Areopagitica*. Macaulay well described Milton's prose as "a perfect field of cloth of gold, rich with gorgeous embroidery;" and, although the prose eloquence of Shelley is not so massive and stately, it is in parts more fervid and impassioned. A severe sentence was passed on a London bookseller, named Eaton, for publishing the third part of Thomas Paine's *Age of Reason*, and this called forth the letter of Shelley referred to, which stands almost unique, considering that the writer of it was only nineteen years of age. In one passage the writer remarks :—" The crime of inquiry is one which religion has never forgiven. Implicit faith and fearless inquiry have in all ages been irreconcilable enemies. Unrestrained philosophy has in every age opposed itself to the reveries of credulity and fanaticism. The truths of astronomy demonstrated by Newton have superseded astrology; since the modern discoveries of chemistry, the philosopher's stone has no longer been deemed attainable. That which is false will ultimately be controverted by its own falsehood." Then, after a closely-reasoned argument, in which he shows that Lord Ellenborough might well fear for the truth of his own opinions, seeing they require such extreme measures to support them, Shelley asks : " Whence is any right derived, but that which power confers, for persecution? Do you think to convert Mr. Eaton to your religion by embittering his existence? You might force him by torture to profess your tenets, but he could not believe them, except you should make them credible, which perhaps exceeds your power. Do you think to please the God you worship by this exhibition of your zeal? If so, the demon to whom some nations offer human hecatombs is less barbarous than the Deity of civilised society. . . . If the law *de hæretico comburendo* has not been formally repealed, I conceive that, from the promise held out by your lordship's zeal, we need not despair of beholding the flames of persecution rekindled in Smithfield. Even now the lash that drove Descartes and Voltaire from their native country, the chains which bound Galileo, the flames which burned Vanini, again resound. . . . Does the Christian God, whom his followers eulogise as the Deity of humility and peace—He, the regenerator of the world, the meek reformer — authorise one man to rise against another, and, because lictors are at his beck, to chain and torture him as an infidel? When the Apostles went abroad to convert the nations, were they enjoined to stab and poison all who disbelieved the divinity of Christ's mission? Assuredly, they

G

would have been no more justifiable in this case
than he is at present who puts into execution the
law which inflicts pillory and imprisonment on
the Deist." It is unnecessary to enlarge in detail
upon the strength and fulness of the invective
to be found in this remarkable pamphlet, or upon
the evidences of great learning it displayed on the
part of its youthful writer; but towards the close
there is the expression of one sentiment which
will find an echo in the present generation, if it
did not in Shelley's. "The time," he says, "is
rapidly approaching—I hope that you, my Lord,
may live to behold its arrival — when the
Mahometan, the Jew, the Christian, the Deist, and
the Atheist will live together in one community,
equally sharing the benefits which arise from its
association, and united in the bonds of charity
and brotherly love." In this aspiration breathes
the catholic spirit of one to whom the very name
of oppression was hateful, and who only needed
to hear of injustice to loathe it from his very
soul.

We perceive, therefore, from what has been
already adduced, that, so far from Shelley declining
the strife of politics, he eagerly rushed into the
fray. If further proofs still were needed, it is
only necessary to refer to his letters to the editors

of the *Statesman* and the *Examiner*, and his espousal of the cause of Mr. Peter Finnerty, the Irish patriot, to whom some slight reference has already been made. With regard to the *Examiner*, most readers will be cognisant of the now historical fact that a conviction was procured against its conductors, John and Leigh Hunt, for writing somewhat too freely upon political topics. Leigh Hunt had referred to the Prince Regent as " this Adonis in loveliness, a corpulent gentleman of fifty;" and if there was one affront more than another which his Royal Highness was likely to resent, it was a reflection upon his august person. There were stronger passages in the libellous article than this description, but none so calculated to bring the Prince into ridicule; and it has always been understood that the real affront consisted in the use of this particular expression; at least, it was believed by many at the time that the article might have been passed over but for these words. Undoubtedly the Prince had been handsome, but his beauty, with all that is lovely, was " fading away," and accordingly the sting of Hunt's remark lay in its plain and unvarnished truth. For the luxury of speaking ironically of the æsthetic appearance of the Regent, the Hunts were sentenced to two years' imprisonment, and were condemned to pay a fine of £1000. We can well understand the kind of feeling this sentence would arouse in Shelley; and it was fully given utterance to in a letter addressed to Mr. Hookham, in which he observes:—"I am boiling with indignation at the horrible injustice and tyranny of the sentence pronounced on Hunt and his brother; and it is on this subject that I write to you. Surely the seal of abjectness and slavery is indelibly stamped upon the character of England. Although I do not retract in the slightest degree my wish for a subscription for the widows and children of those poor men hung at York, yet this £1000 which the Hunts are sentenced to pay is an affair of more consequence. Hunt is a brave, a good, and an enlightened man. Surely the public, for whom Hunt has done so much, will repay in part the great debt of obligation which they owe the champion of their liberties and virtues; or are they dead, cold, stone-hearted, and insensible— brutalised by centuries of unremitting bondage? However that may be, they surely may be ex- cited into some slight acknowledgment of his merits. Whilst hundreds of thousands are sent to the tyrants of Russia, he pines in a dungeon, far from all that can make life desired." Shelley encloses a cheque, and exclaims, " Oh, that I might

wallow for one night in the Bank of England!"
Whatever may be said of the visionary character
of Shelley's projects, his sympathy with, and
earnestness in, political reforms and causes were
intense in the extreme.

In considering Shelley as a politician, we cannot
but take cognisance of a pamphlet which he
issued on the subject of Parliamentary Reform,
under the signature of the "Hermit of Marlow."
This was neither more nor less than a proposal for
putting reform to the vote throughout the kingdom.
The writer's views are expressed in very moderate
language, and though personally an extreme Radical, there evidently dwelt in his mind at the
time he wrote the pamphlet an idea that he could
not expect to gain immediately for the world all
the freedom which might be desirable. The work
is consequently careful and statesmanlike in its
arrangement. The gist of the proposals was that
committees should be formed with a view to polling
the entire people on the subject which was then
agitating all circles, as it has done at set periods
during the whole of this century. Shelley did not
regard it as just and equitable that the people should
be governed by laws, and impoverished by taxes,
originating in the edicts of an assembly which represented somewhat less than a thousandth part of

the entire community. He therefore drew up six Resolutions to be submitted to a national meeting of the friends of reform. These resolutions set forth that all persons who were of opinion that reform was necessary in parliamentary representation, should assemble themselves together for the purpose of collecting evidence as to how far it was the will of the majority of the nation to move in the exercise of their rights; that the whole population should be canvassed in favour of a declaration that the House of Commons does not represent the will of the nation; that meetings should be held day after day for the reception of evidence bearing upon the subject; that the reformers disclaimed any design of lending their sanction to revolutionary and disorganising schemes; and that a subscription be set on foot to defray the expenses of the plan. Shelley then proceeds to state in detail the reforms which he considers necessary, and foremost amongst these is a recommendation on behalf of annual parliaments. The pamphlet closes with this very remarkable passage :—" With respect to universal suffrage, I confess I consider its adoption, in the present unprepared state of public feeling and knowledge, a measure fraught with peril. *I think that none but those who register their names as paying a certain small sum in direct*

taxes ought at present to send members to Parliament.
The consequence of the immediate extension of
the elective franchise to every male adult would
be to place power in the hands of men who have
been rendered brutal and torpid and ferocious by
ages of slavery.   It is to suppose that the qualities
belonging to a demagogue are such as are sufficient
to endow a legislator.   I allow Major Cartwright's
arguments to be unanswerable; abstractedly, it is
the right of every human being to have a share in
the Government.   But Mr. Paine's arguments are
also unanswerable; a pure republic may be shown,
by inferences the most obvious and irresistible, to
be that system of social order the fittest to produce
the happiness and promote the genuine eminence
of man.   Yet nothing less consists with reason, or
affords smaller hopes of beneficial issue, than the
plan which should abolish the regal and the
aristocratical branches of our Constitution, before
the public mind, through many gradations of
improvement, shall have arrived at the maturity
which can disregard these symbols of its childhood."
I apprehend that this extract effectually disposes
of the ignorant assumption that Shelley knew
nothing whatever of politics; on the contrary,
there were few living in his own day who could
have put in fewer words a better idea of the ideal

state of government and the obstacles which intervene to prevent its realisation. The basis of
representation indicated in the sentence in italics
was long afterwards almost the very groundwork
of the Parliamentary Reform Bill carried by the
present Premier in 1867, as Mr. Rossetti also has
observed in his Memoir of the poet. Not only
must Shelley have studied politics, but, *pace* Mr.
Hogg, he must have studied them with something
more than a superficial observation, or for the sole
purpose of enlarging glibly upon them. His
writing on political subjects is as far-seeing as
anything he has left behind him, with the exception of certain of his poems, and in them we naturally look for the prophet of the race.

Another evidence of Shelley's devotion to
political problems, and of his thorough delight in
grappling with them, is seen in his "Declaration
of Rights," which Mr. Rossetti points out resembles
"the two most famous of similar documents in the
history of the great French Revolution—the one
adopted by the Constituent Assembly in August
1789, and the other proposed in April 1793 by
Robespierre." In Shelley's "Declaration," which
seems to have been foreshadowed to a certain
extent by his "Proposals for an Association"
already remarked upon, we are struck with the

terseness and vigour of the various affirmations. Consider a few of them for their exhibition of sound judgment and wisdom :—"Government has no rights; it is a delegation from several individuals for the purpose of securing their own. It is, there-fore, just only so far as it exists by their consent, useful only so far as it operates to their well-being." "As the benefit of the governed is, or ought to be, the origin of government, no men can have any authority that does not expressly emanate from their will." "No man has a right to disturb the public peace by personally resisting the execution of a law, however bad. He ought to acquiesce, using at the same time the utmost powers of his reason to promote its repeal." "A man has a right to unrestricted liberty of discussion." "False-hood is a scorpion that will sting itself to death." "A man has not only a right to express his thoughts, but it is his duty to do so." "Expediency is inadmissible in morals. Politics are only sound when conducted on principles of morality; they are, in fact, the morals of nations." "Belief is in-voluntary; nothing involuntary is meritorious or reprehensible. A man ought not to be considered worse or better for his belief." "A Christian, a Deist, a Turk, and a Jew have equal rights; they are men and brethren." "If a person's religious

ideas correspond not with your own, love him
nevertheless.　Those who believe that Heaven is,
what earth has been, a monopoly in the hands of
a favoured few, would do well to reconsider their
opinion; if they find that it came from their priest
or their grandmother, they could not do better
than reject it." "The only use of government is
to repress the vices of man.　If man were to-day
sinless, to-morrow he would have a right to
demand that government and all its evils should
cease."　In the light of these apothegms we perceive why Shelley was dreaded and detested by
many in his own generation.　His views, as thus expressed, might have extracted the admiration of a
Plato, but were only calculated to sting the aver-
age English politician of the nineteenth century
into indignation.　What can there be in common
between the holder of such pure and just views as
those enunciated in these maxims and the man
who buys his seat in the legislature by the most
wholesale and unblushing bribery?　Politically, it
may be said that Shelley is summed up by two
broad distinguishing characteristics, viz.—a love of
freedom, and his convictions in favour of an enlightened republic.　Mrs. Shelley dilates upon his
love of the people, and his ardent admiration of
the idea of equality, and observes that "he looked

on political freedom as the direct agent to effect the happiness of mankind." His biographer, Medwin, has endeavoured to prove that he was somewhat of a lukewarm Republican, but is not very successful in his effort; indeed, he is compelled to admit that "Shelley used to say that a republic was the best form of government, with disinterestedness, abnegation of self, and a Spartan virtue; but to produce which required the black bread and soup of the Lacedæmonians, an equality of fortunes unattainable in the present factitious state of society, and only to be brought about by an agrarian law, and a consequent baptism of blood." In politics Shelley knew no fear. And so thoroughly conscientious was he in giving action to his views, and so ardent a Radical, that he would probably have abjured the dignity of a baronet had it ever been his fortune to succeed to the title. This view is strengthened by the knowledge that, in season and out of season, he never refrained from insisting upon one great cardinal principle or doctrine, viz.—that no man had a right to enjoy benefits, or the goodwill of the world, unless these sprang from the exercise of virtue and talent. He could not have been a fair-weather politician, that is, one who croaks republicanism till he gets a stake in the country, and then becomes that

worst of all Conservatives, an embodiment of selfishness; this is proved from the fact that immediately he inherited wealth he proceeded to distribute.
it in a lavish and possibly injudicious manner.
Speaking generally, of course, it may be said that
Shelley's political views were such as had been
formulated in the systems of Paine and Godwin;
but Shelley was Paine and Godwin with a large
heart added; and, certainly, while he was strengthened by their countenance, his own political conceptions were self-derived, and a necessity—partly
by reason of his mental constitution, and partly as
the result of his personal experience.   Shelley's
politics grew with his growth; he had an innate
sense of political justice and a burning desire for
equality; and those would do his spirit wrong who
could imagine that any circumstances of possible
worldly success, or the dazzling possession of rank,
could ever have caused him to apostatise from the
simplicity of his political faith.

Was Shelley an atheist ? Such is the momentous
question which next arises.   The affirmative has
so frequently been stated that it has come to be
almost universally accepted.   I, also, believe that
he had not quite dived into the depth of all mystery;
that he had not fully understood himself, the
world, and the Great Unknown; that he had not

quite reconciled all the inconsistencies of this jarring instrument, human life, nor solved the problem why evil should be permitted to exist side by side with virtue, and too frequently prove the victor. But then he never professed to be anything but a student upon the threshold of existence, possessed by a thirst for knowledge. Yet, assuming for a moment that at one time Shelley was of the number of the sceptics, there was an earnestness in his purposes, and a craving for light, which were noble in comparison with the cold Mephistophelean disbelief in virtue so characteristic of Byron. The author of *Queen Mab* was a man of faith compared with the author of *Don Juan*. Out of the spirit of inquiry which pervaded the former it was possible there might arise a sympathy with and a thirsting after the Divine; out of the spirit of moral infidelity which distinguished the latter it was impossible for anything to be generated but a distrust in all human virtue. So that our words of indignation as regards Shelley's scepticism should be measured and sympathetic, not violent and unsparing. The negations of a philosophical scepticism have in the world's history very frequently been cast away for a living and vital trust in the Fountain of all happiness and truth. Morality always survived in Shelley; therefore it

was possible for him, by an easy and natural
process, to pass from the lower and baser to the
higher and nobler. Shelleyism is not infidelity;
and if systematic doubt really ever was a creed
with the poet, it had been swept away long before
his death. We can distinguish Shelley stretching
out hands of faith after the Divine, imploring,
demanding to be led into the light, and seeking
shelter in the Fatherhood of his Creator. Are not
these eloquent lines one of the finest tributes
which could be cited to the power of the Divine
Nazarene ?—

> " A Power from the unknown God,
>   A Promethean conqueror came ;
>   Like a triumphal path he trod
>   The thorns of death and shame.
>   A mortal shape to him
>   Was like the vapour dim
>   Which the orient planet animates with light :
>   Hell, sin, and slavery came,
>   Like bloodhounds mild and tame,
>   Nor preyed until their lord had taken flight.
>   The moon of Mahomet
>   Arose, and it shall set :
>   While blazoned as on Heaven's immortal noon,
>   The Cross leads generations on."

The scepticism which Shelley indulged was not
one of utter disbelief in the future perfection of
humanity, but one that had its root in the sad-

ness he experienced for a world which was apparently without a guiding principle, or power; and in regret for the transitoriness of everything human. He looked abroad with the sadly-brooding eyes of the poet, and wept over the absence of that stability in some person or thing which his soul longed to have revealed. Earth to him was a land of shadows, and men " as clouds that veil the midnight moon." As he sorrowfully affirms, "Nought may endure but mutability."

A priest at Lausanne once gesticulated on reading *Queen Mab*, " Infidel, Jacobine, leveller; nothing can stop this spread of blasphemy but the stake and the faggot; the world is retrograding into accursed heathenism and universal anarchy." It was seeing so much of the spirit which animated this priest that retarded Shelley's religious development. But, with every consideration for the Lausanne clerical —whose bigotry too often finds its exemplification in each succeeding age—another critic of Shelley's, in humbler life, a simple bookseller, was nearer to the truth when he remarked that Shelley aimed at regenerating, not levelling mankind, as Byron and Moore. The detestation of the name of religion which he at one time unquestionably displayed arose from the lack of the thing itself in those who professed it. He looked upon religion, as practised, "as hostile instead of friendly to the cultivation of those virtues which would make men brothers." From the poem of *Queen Mab* it is impossible to come to the conclusion that Shelley was an atheist, except as regards the God too often represented as the God of vengeance by the Christians, whom indeed he rejects with scorn. But there are glimmerings of a belief in some Power which moulds all things and runs through all things—in fact a Pantheistic God. To the God of the theologians he exhibited an unswerving animosity; but the pamphlet he wrote at Oxford was much more atheistical than the poem. There is abundant evidence, notwithstanding, that in after life he abjured both the pamphlet and the poem. By far the most reckless things Shelley ever wrote are to be found in the notes to *Queen Mab*, but here, appended to the quotation from the poem, "There is no God!" we find him saying, "This negation must be understood solely to affect a creative Deity. The hypothesis of a pervading spirit, co-eternal with the Universe, remains unshaken." This is an admission which no man who was an atheist in the strict sense of the term would make. As one fact is worth many arguments, however, I would again remind the reader that in his letter to the Editor of the *Examiner* on the subject of *Queen Mab*,

Shelley said the poem was never intended for publication; and that, as we have seen, in regard to the subtle discriminations of metaphysical and religious doctrine, it was very crude and immature. It was written at a period when the poet was disgusted with the constitution of things, and when he was desirous of hurling from his throne the Deity whom Christians held up for reverence. He repudiated the notion that this Being described to him could be the active Governor of the universe. At the same time he did believe distinctly in some Spirit that was progressively working for perfection. These views are corroborated by Shelley's reply to Trelawny, when the latter asked, "Why do you call yourself an atheist?" and he answered, "I used it (the name atheist) to express my abhorrence of superstition: I took up the word, as a knight took up a gauntlet, in defiance of injustice." This is a clear indication of the character of Shelley's atheism; it was, as I have maintained, not a universal negative. The very spirituality of his nature would have prevented him from embracing the everlasting "No!"

Coleridge took this view of the poet's opinions, for in one of his letters he observes, "His (Shelley's) discussions—tending towards atheism of a certain sort—would not have scared *me*; for *me* it would have been a semi-transparent larva, soon to be glorified, and through which I should have seen the true image,—the final metamorphosis. Besides, I have ever thought that sort of atheism the next best religion to Christianity; nor does the better faith I have learnt from Paul and John interfere with the cordial reverence I feel for Benedict Spinoza."   I find also this remarkable passage in a letter written by Shelley himself, in 1811 ;—" I here take God (God exists) to witness that I wish torments, which beggar the futile description of a fancied hell, would fall upon me, provided I could obtain thereby that happiness for *what* I love, which, I fear, can never be ! The question is, What do I love ?   It is almost unnecessary to answer.   Do I love the person, the embodied identity, if I may be allowed the expression ?   No ! I love what is superior, what is excellent, or what I conceive to be so ; and I wish, ardently wish, to be profoundly convinced of the existence of a Deity, that so superior a spirit might receive some degree of happiness from my feeble exertions ; for love is heaven, and heaven is love. You think so too, and you disbelieve not the existence of an eternal, omnipresent Spirit."   Then, in an argument against the Materialists, the writer proceeds further to say, " I think I can prove the existence of a Deity—a First Cause.   I will ask a

Materialist how came this universe at first? He will answer, By chance. What chance? I will answer in the words of Spinoza : ' An infinite number of atoms had been floating from all eternity in space, till at last one of them fortuitously diverged from its track, which dragging with it another formed the principle of gravitation, and, in consequence, the universe! What cause produced this change, this chance? For where do we know that causes arise without their correspondent effects; at least we must here, on so abstract a subject, reason analogically. Was not this, then, a *cause*, was it not a *first* cause? Was not this first cause a Deity? Now, nothing remains but to prove that this Deity has a care, or rather that its only employment consists in regulating the present and future happiness of its creation. Our ideas of infinite space, etc., are scarcely to be called ideas, for we cannot either comprehend or explain them; therefore the Deity must be judged by us from attributes analogical to our situation.' Oh, that this Deity were the Soul of the universe, the spirit of universal, imperishable love! Indeed, it is." This is certainly language never held by an atheist; it was the expression of a man in doubt about the truths of Christianity, but not that of an unbeliever. Phrases occur in several poems by Shelley, which touch upon the same

thoughts as those developed in this prose extract.
On one occasion, it is true, he said, "I had rather
be damned with Plato and Lord Bacon than go to
heaven with Paley and Malthus;" but this was
only to indicate his abhorrence of creeds and formulated religions.   Yet he held the view which
is common to almost all Christians—viz. that evil
was not originally inherent in the creation, but an
alien element that might be expelled.   Every student of Shelley must perceive that he had a deeply
religious spirit, that spirit of reverence which invariably distinguishes the great poet; for would it not
be impossible to conceive of a great poet who was
at the same time an atheist?   He would at once
lose that spiritual elevation which refines and
glorifies genius.   The best description of the religious attitude of Shelley has been given by one
who knew him most intimately, and as I greatly
prefer his language to my own, in enforcing the point
now at issue, his words shall be reproduced.

" The leading feature of Shelley's character,"
says Leigh Hunt, who may be credited with having
understood more than others the thoughts of his
later life, " may be said to have been a natural
piety.   He did himself injustice with the public,
in using the popular name of the Supreme Being
inconsiderately.   He identified it solely with the

most vulgar and tyrannical notions of a God made after the worst human fashion; and did not sufficiently reflect that it was often used by a juster devotion to express a sense of the Great Mover of the universe. An impatience in contradicting worldly and pernicious notions of a supernatural power led his own aspirations to be misunderstood; for, though in the severity of his dialectics, and particularly in moments of despondency, he sometimes appeared to be hopeless of what he most desired—and though he justly thought that a Divine Being would prefer the increase of benevolence and good before any praise, or even recognition of himself (a reflection worth thinking of by the intolerant), yet, in reality, there was no belief to which he clung with more fondness than that of some great pervading 'Spirit of Intellectual Beauty;' as may be seen in his aspirations on that subject. He assented warmly to an opinion which I expressed in the Cathedral at Pisa, while the organ was playing, that a truly divine religion might yet be established, if charity were really made the principle of it instead of faith." But in discussing this subject it is necessary to take into account Shelley's *Essay on Christianity*, in which I find him distinctly asserting that "we are not the creators of our own origin and existence.

We are not the arbiters of every motion of our
own complicated nature; we are not the masters
of our own imaginations and moods of mental
being. There is a Power by which we are surrounded, like the atmosphere in which some motion-
less lyre is suspended, which visits with its breath
our silent chords at will." In this same essay
there is a nobler tribute to Jesus Christ than
many of the cold believers in Christianity, dead
with an infidelity of heart, would be willing to pay.
The whole spirit of the essay forbids for a moment
the assumption that Shelley was an atheist, and
most of the composition might be read with great
profit from any orthodox pulpit. On other col-
lateral religious questions, such as the doctrine of
the immortality of the soul, much is not said by
Shelley. Immortality is a topic rarely discussed
with himself by any man, and when he becomes
agitated therewith it is only to end in a condition
of vagueness. Yet the expectation of something
after death was very strong in Shelley. *Adonais*,
if it stood alone as regards the poet's utterances
on immortality, might be conclusive of his belief
in the doctrine in its fullest sense; in speaking of
Keats, in one instance he says that "he hath
awakened from the dream of life," and "is made
one with Nature." Further, that his spirit "beams

from the abode where the Eternal are." Other
prose expressions of Shelley's would appear to
contradict this, but never, I believe, does he hint
for a moment at such a thing as annihilation.
He could not conceive that his own spirit, after
the experience of which he was conscious, could ever
be thrown into the void, useless and dead, though
he had no definite ideas as to what would become
of himself after he "had shuffled off this mortal
coil." By this time has he not discovered more
fully that Divine love for which his spirit yearned ?
Had a few more years of human life been allotted
to him, he would have emerged from that dark
valley of doubt in which his noble spirit was
searching for the Infinite. The light, however,
came more suddenly; the veil of humanity was
violently rent asunder, and Shelley was face to
face with the solution of the Great Mystery.

The benefactor of humanity has invariably to
sustain much comment respecting his motives, and
Shelley was no exception to the rule in his exercise of the spirit of philanthropy. He gave both
of his labour and substance with an unbounded
generosity, and too frequently had the bitterness
to perceive that his intentions were misunderstood,
and he himself regarded with suspicion. Man is
certainly a reasoning animal, but he is above all a

selfish animal. The species seems much more prolific and ingenious in acts of self-preservation than
it does in argument. Man is, in fact, so selfish
that an undoubtedly benevolent act—an act, that
is, which is open to no other construction—too oft
surprises him by its folly. He furthermore does
not like the rebuke which the act itself necessarily
conveys, and consequently becomes angry, and
slanders his benefactor. This has ever been so.
In the realms of thought and science, as well as
in personal action, the exercise of benevolence has
met with strenuous opposition. The perfect Man,
whose soul was spotless, and who yearned with a
magnificent philanthropy over the whole race, was
crucified on a tree. The world has to be ap-
proached gradually by the philanthropist, or he
will be assailed by the offensive missiles of an
adverse criticism. And when he has done all the
good that is possible, and laid down his life for his
brother, he will gain but a grudging remembrance
from posterity. It is, however, the mark of the
true philanthropist that he pursues his ends re-
gardless of the consequences. No threat, no with-
holding of his just reward, can ever deter him, for
he is armed, not by the principle which expects a
return for its expended benevolence, but by the
sublime idea that the condition of the person he

means to help can be ameliorated and exalted by his aid. And in the eyes of the philanthropist the salvation of the species is the noblest work to which a man can devote himself. Salvation from vice, from misery, from poverty, from the horrors of his own conscience, is to the human the lifting up of the Divine ideal. Of Shelley it may be affirmed that he laboured conspicuously for this end. The record of his life is one of generous impulse and action from its commencement to its close. A benignity and reverence, worthy of all praise, animated him in his relations to man and the humbler creation; to breathe, to him, was to aspire to do good, irrespective of recognition or reward. His own appetites were conquered and held in subjection, so that he could be of service to humanity. The plainest food sufficed for his daily needs, and he would never use the produce of the cane so long as it was obtained by slave labour. "Fragile in health and frame; of the purest habits in morals; full of devoted generosity and universal kindness; glowing with ardour to obtain wisdom; resolved, at every personal sacrifice, to do right; burning with a desire for affection and sympathy, he was treated as a reprobate, cast forth as a criminal." Lest this eulogy, however, which was dictated by the

spirit of an ardent love and admiration for Shelley,
should seem tinged with the extravagance of
personal regard, let us quote from Lady Blessington
what Lord Byron said of his friend. After Shelley's
death his lordship wrote—" You should have
known Shelley to feel how much I must regret
him. He was the most gentle, the most amiable,
the least worldly-minded person I ever met; full
of delicacy, disinterested beyond all other men,
and possessing a degree of genius joined to a
simplicity as rare as it is admirable. He had
formed to himself a *beau idéal* of all that is fine,
high-minded, and noble, and he acted up to this
ideal even to the very letter. He had a most
brilliant imagination, but a total want of worldly
wisdom. I have seen nothing like him, and never
shall again, I am certain." To extract such a
tribute from such a quarter is of itself sufficient
proof to me that all I have alleged with respect
to the natural generosity of Shelley's character is
strictly accurate.

A munificent instance of this trait in the poet's
disposition was afforded during his stay in North
Wales. He had hired a cottage from a gentleman
named Maddox, at Tanyrallt, Carnarvonshire.
Mr. Maddox, Lady Shelley informs us, had re-
claimed several thousand acres of land from the

sea; but the embankment proved insufficient during an unusually high tide. The sea made such serious breaches in the earthworks that the poor cottagers became terribly alarmed. At this juncture Shelley stepped forward, took the matter up warmly, and personally solicited subscriptions from the gentlemen of the neighbourhood. Though possessing very limited means of subsistence himself, he headed the list with the extraordinary donation of £500. Nor was his enthusiasm checked here, for he came up to London, still interested in the same business, and had at length the satisfaction of seeing his efforts crowned with success. The embankment was repaired and strengthened, and the inhabitants were protected from future risk.

Leigh Hunt, in his *Autobiography*, tells a story of another kind, but in excellent illustration of the same tenderness of heart. On returning home to Hampstead one night after the opera, Hunt heard strange and alarming shrieks mixed with the voice of a man. It appears that it was a fierce winter night, and Shelley had found a woman lying near the top of the hill, in fits. He tried in vain to get the nearest householders to receive her, assuring them that she was no impostor: doors were shut upon him. Time was flying, and the poor creature was in convulsions, with her son lamenting over her. Seeing a carriage drive up to a door and a gentleman with his family step out of it, Shelley implored them to have mercy on the woman. In response to his request that the gentleman would go and see her, the latter said, "No, sir; there's no necessity for that sort of thing, depend on it. Impostors swarm everywhere; the thing cannot be done; sir, your conduct is extraordinary." "Sir," cried Shelley, "I am sorry to say that your conduct is not extraordinary; and if my own seems to amaze you, I will tell you something which may amaze you a little more, and I hope will frighten you. It is such men as you who madden the spirits and the patience of the poor and the wretched; and if ever a convulsion comes in this country (which is very probable) recollect what I tell you: you will have your house, that you refuse to put the miserable woman into, burnt over your head." Then, as Dr. Johnson rescued a wretched creature on a similar memorable occasion, the poet, as best he was able, conveyed the suffering woman to a haven of rest. Thus this man lived, who was so subject to violent bodily pains that he was sometimes compelled to lie on the ground during the paroxysms of suffering; yet preserving always the language of kindness and consideration for those about him. To multiply the record of his generous deeds would be to follow the diary of his whole existence. So strongly imbued was he with the desire to do good, that he compelled any recreation or occupation to give way when there was opened before him an avenue for benevolence. After pecuniary circumstances became a little easier with him than they had been, Shelley went to reside at Great Marlow. Mrs. Shelley has, in a few lines, detailed how he spent his life there. It appears that, though Marlow was surrounded by every natural beauty, it boasted of a very poor population. "The women," says Mrs. Shelley, "were lacemakers, and lost their health by sedentary labour, for which they were very ill paid. The poor-laws ground to the dust, not only the paupers, but those who had risen just above that state, and were obliged to pay poor-rates. The changes produced by peace following a long war and a bad harvest brought with them the most heart-rending evils to the poor. Shelley afforded what alleviation he could. In the winter, while bringing out his poem (*The Revolt of Islam*) he had a severe attack of ophthalmia, caught while visiting the poor cottagers." And there was no calling out for strangers to come and see the good deeds which he wrought. All sprang from the purest motives, and he shrank from having his actions blazoned abroad. Occasionally, nevertheless, he assisted friends in the pursuit of schemes which were chimerical, and which would have been better left alone; but when the friend was invoked in time of need, he was only too ready to respond to the call, whatever it might be. I have made a passing reference to his sympathy for the brute creation, which was such that any instance of cruelty put him into transports of passion. One such case is recorded in his Memoirs, and this incident is but typical. Of the broader kind of philanthropy which seeks to benefit the race, and not specially the individual, Shelley also gave many demonstrations; but one fact must suffice—viz., that long before the abolition of the punishment of death had become a moot question, Shelley had firmly cherished the idea. He advocated it upon the same grounds as Dickens—many years subsequently—to wit, that it served no good or useful purpose to society, and was contrary to the spirit of human progress.

In leaving this portion of the subject, I cannot refrain from quoting a portion of an article which appeared in the *Examiner* of October 10, 1819, which testifies alike to the simplicity of Shelley's life and his philanthropic spirit. A reviewer in the *Quarterly* had asserted that the poet was "shamefully dissolute in his conduct." Meeting this infamous charge—which, to those who really knew Shelley, required no contradiction—the writer in the *Examiner* (Leigh Hunt) said: "We heard of similar assertions when we resided in the same house with Mr. Shelley for nearly three months; and how was he living all that time? As much like Plato himself, as all his theories resemble Plato—or rather still more like a Pythagorean. This was the round of his daily life—he was up early, breakfasted sparingly, wrote at the *Revolt of Islam* all the morning, went out in his boat, or into the woods with some Greek author or the Bible in his hands; came home to a dinner of vegetables (for he took neither meat nor wine), visited, if necessary, the sick and fatherless, whom others gave Bibles to and no help, wrote or studied again, or read to his wife and friends the whole evening; took a crust of bread or a glass of whey for his supper, and went early to bed. This is literally the whole of the life he led, or that we believe he now leads in Italy; nor have we ever known him, in spite of the malignant and ludicrous exaggerations on this point, deviate, notwithstanding his theories, even into a single action which those who differ from him might think blameable. We do not say that he would always square his conduct by their opinions as a matter of principle, we only say that he acted just as if he did so square it. We forbear, out of regard for the very bloom of their beauty, to touch upon numberless other charities and generosities which we have known him exercise; but this we must say in general, that we never lived with a man who gave so complete an idea of an ardent and principled aspirant in philosophy as Percy Shelley, and that we believe him from the bottom of our hearts to be one of the noblest hearts as well as heads which the world has seen for a long time. We never met, in short, with a being who came nearer, perhaps so near, to that height of humanity mentioned in the conclusion of an essay of Lord Bacon's, where he speaks of excess of charity, and of its not being in the power of man or angel to come in danger by it." Such is the Shelley of real life.

We have thus completed another stage in the consideration of this illustrious friend of humanity. I have expressed my own unwavering admiration of the various aspects of his character, and the triple view of him now presented may assist, possibly, in elucidating to others a career which is at once romantic, beautiful, and tragic. That career forcibly rebukes the idea that enthusiasm and personal sacrifice are necessarily divorced from the selfish and materially progressive age in which we live. The theologian may well merge his wrath in the halo of practical Christianity which encircled this life; the adamantine creed is worthless and dead before his sleepless and laborious devotion. In Divine hands we can leave him, resenting the bigotry and the presumption which would pass judgment upon him here. If that soul which possessed so much purity, grace, disinterestedness, and sincerity could be ultimately lost, the foundations of our faith might well be in danger of being broken up. But the speculation is at once impossible and impious: the Deity himself is pledged to the imperishable nature of goodness and virtue.

III.

LATER YEARS AND OPINIONS.

> " Thou art fled
> Like some frail exhalation, which the dawn
> Robes in its golden beams—ah ! thou hast fled !
> The brave, the gentle, and the beautiful,
> The child of grace and genius."
>
> *Alastor.*

LATER YEARS AND OPINIONS.

Two of the most tragic events in the history of English literature—one occurring at the dawn of the most famous age in that literature, and the other at the beginning of the present century,—deprived the world of two great luminaries in the realm of poetry. On the 1st of June 1593, Christopher Marlowe, greatest of the founders of the English drama before Shakspeare, was stabbed by one Francis Archer in a tavern at Deptford, and died of his wounds: on the 8th of July 1822, during a storm of only twenty minutes' duration, a little craft, bearing Percy Bysshe Shelley on board, went down in the Bay of Spezzia, and was afterwards tossed tenantless on shore. These distinguished poets, at the time of their death, might have been regarded as only upon the threshold of existence, for neither had quite attained his thirtieth year, and notwithstanding the opposite character of their lives,

there yet existed considerable affinity between
their spirits.   In storm and tempest they lived,
and under the same conditions they passed away.
Both were branded with the name of atheist.
Turbulent, and given to excess with many of his
brethren of the Elizabethan era, rare and divine
poetic fancies passed athwart the vision of Marlowe, and similar inspirations visited the later poet.
The life of Shelley was of a higher and nobler type
than that of the early dramatist; but between the
author of *Dr. Faustus* and the author of *The
Cenci* there was, as I have intimated, not a little
in common.   United to the same wayward, generous, and impulsive nature was a kindred imagination, thrown, in the case of Marlowe, into the
dramatic form, in obedience to the spirit of the
genius of the period; Shelley, tortured almost into
madness by that very civilisation into whose
midst he was cast, poured out the burden of his woe
and his anger in any and every form of verse
which seemed meet to his soul, so greatly suffering
and perturbed.   But ceasing at this point to pursue whatever analogy may exist between the
Hercules of the sixteenth century and the far-off
genius of the nineteenth, let us now concern our-
selves with the later years of Shelley, distinguishing, if possible, their effect upon his literary work.

In M. Taine's able survey of English Literature
—a work, nevertheless, disfigured by many defects
—the author appears in one passage to read the
character and work of Shelley with keen penetration. After sketching the brief and troubled life
of the poet, and demanding whether it is not a
type of the genuine bard and prophet, he proceeds
to observe that for souls constituted in a mould
like his, the great consolation is Nature. "Has
any one since Shakspeare and Spenser lighted on
such tender and such grand ecstasies? Has any-
one painted so magnificently the cloud which
watches by night in the sky, enveloping in its net
the swarm of golden bees, the stars?" These are
some of the inquiries of the French critic, and our
sympathies accompany him till this extract is
reached, which may be regarded as a fair specimen
of his occasionally unsound rhetoric,—"It is this
presentiment and yearning which sustains all
modern poetry—now in Christian meditations, as
with Campbell and Wordsworth, now in pagan
visions, as with Keats and Shelley. They hear
the great heart of Nature beat; they wish to reach
it; they try all spiritual and sensible approaches,
through Judea and through Greece, by consecrated
doctrines, and by prescribed dogmas. In this
splendid and fruitless effort the greatest become

exhausted and die. Their poetry, which they drag
with them over these sublime tracts, is torn to
pieces. One alone, Byron, attains the summit;
and of all these grand poetic draperies, which
float like banners, and seem to summon men to
the conquest of supreme truth, we see now but
tatters scattered by the wayside." A fallacy lies
embedded here; for surely a protest must be
entered against the assumption that Byron soared
to the altitude of the full-orbed poet, while Wordsworth, with the treasures of his *Excursion*, and
Shelley, with all his splendid flights of imagination, were but the dispensers of fragments of song.
On two occasions, in *Prometheus Unbound* and *The
Cenci*, Shelley almost rose to the great height of perfect and complete spiritual and dramatic vision—a
height to which Byron, notwithstanding the vigour
of his genius, never fully attained. But the principal point to which observation should be directed
is, that the inability to discover satisfaction in the
mere contemplation of human life threw Shelley,
as it were, into the bosom of Nature, and led to
his seclusion from the world. He had passed
through bitter experience of humanity; he had
been animated with zeal for its welfare, and fired by
quixotic schemes for its redemption from error and
prejudice; but the world had ill-repaid its sanguine

apostle and would-be deliverer. Instead of hailing his ideal schemes for its progress and development, it had hurled the javelin into the most secret recesses of his nature. He had been sore wounded through the domestic affections—trials producing a revulsion in his sensitive nature; and we have now to deal with him, disabused, to a large extent, of his faith in himself to hasten the regeneration of the world, and falling back upon the material beauty and magnificence of the universe for the sustenance of his ever-yearning and aspiring spirit.

In the year 1816, Shelley was in Switzerland, having made the acquaintance of Lord Byron at Geneva. The passionate fondness of both poets for the water is well known, and one incident is related which was a faint foreshadowing of the terrible event that occurred some years later. Shelley and Byron were sailing from Meillerie to St. Gingoux when a storm came on, and the vessel shipped a good deal of water. Here was manifested the unselfish current of Shelley's nature. Being unable to swim, he made up his mind, under the most heroic calm, to the death which appeared inevitable; in fact he said he had no notion of being saved, and was determined not to allow Byron to imperil his own life by attempting to save him. Fortunately, after much difficulty, the boat righted, and the world was largely the gainer by this propitious circumstance. This temper of fearlessness in presence of the very article of death, which distinguished the ancients much more than the moderns, was very characteristic of Shelley. In all circumstances involving personal danger he was as unconscious and devoid of fear as a child. Numberless anecdotes could be told illustrative of this phase of his character. His moral courage also, as well as his physical, was pre-eminent. By no persuasion or entreaty could he be brought to say that a thing was other, in the least degree, than the complexion of which he thought. He cut invariably at the root of all things, and was absolutely fearless in the expression of his views, upon all occasions, and under all conditions. Inconvenient as this attitude might sometimes be, viewed in the light of one's relations towards the outer world, it unquestionably relieves him who adopts it from much circumlocution, and not a little of that veneer so prevalent in all classes of society.

Mrs. Shelley's opinion that during the early stages of Shelley's friendship with Byron, his genius was in some measure checked by his association with the author of *Childe Harold*, whose nature was utterly dissimilar to his own, is both natural and probable. But if Byron endeavoured to make Shelley more in love with the real, there was also a reflex action upon himself proceeding from the more ethereal and spiritualised poet. Moore has fully testified to this in his *Memorials of Lord Byron*. Although there was scarcely a point of agreement between the two men when they came to discuss philosophy and poetry, in time the influence of Shelley upon Byron was palpable and distinct. " Upon no point," we are reminded, " were the opposite tendencies of the two friends—to long-established opinions and matter-of-fact on one side, and to all that was most innovating and visionary on the other—more observable than in their notions on philosophical subjects ; Lord Byron being, with the great bulk of mankind, a believer in the existence of matter and evil, while Shelley so far refined upon the theory of Berkeley, as not only to resolve the whole of creation into spirit, but to add also to this inmaterial system some pervading principle, some abstract nonentity of love and beauty, of which—as a substitute, at least, for Deity—the philosophic bishop had never dreamed. On such subjects, and on poetry, their conversation generally turned ; and as might be expected from Lord Byron's facility in receiving new impressions, the opinions of his companion were not altogether without some influence on his mind." Shelley's detachment from men and the material side of things was curiously described by himself in a letter to a friend respecting his *Epipsychidion.* He says—" The *Epipsychidion* is a mystery; as to real flesh and blood you know that I do not deal in those articles; you might as well go to a gin-shop for a leg of mutton, as expect anything human or earthly from me." It is said that Shelley, when with Byron, felt somewhat oppressed by the weight of what he conceived to be his friend's superior poetical powers; and yet there is no doubt that Shelley influenced Byron more than the latter influenced Shelley. There was a certain grandeur in Shelley's nature, which, combined with his intense earnestness and spirituality, must have left a strong if not always clearly traceable impression upon the grosser nature of Byron. Notwithstanding this influence, however, it is scarcely matter for surprise that Shelley should have failed to convert Byron completely from that love of materiality, which was his strong bias both of body and soul. But it is pleasant to know that the generous championship of Wordsworth on the part of Shelley caused Byron to revise and greatly modify his opinion of the poet of the Lakes. From a reviler he passed, indeed, at one time, into a partial imitator of Wordsworth.

In a letter written from Ravenna, some years after their first meeting, Byron addresses Shelley upon literary subjects, and takes occasion to refer to Keats's ultra-sensitiveness. It is curious to note the difference in poets in this respect. Adverse criticism produced in Byron rage and rebelliousness; in Shelley sadness and pity; in Keats a temporary despair, if not a permanent feeling akin to that. The idea, once so common, that Keats was absolutely "snuffed out by an article," and that he died of a broken heart, has recently been exploded; but it is not impossible that the severity of his critics may have given an impetus to that insidious disease of which he died. Keats had a proud and sensitive soul, and in all probability suffered more from the literary on-slaughts upon him than he was willing to confess to his friends. It is in the nature of such poets to cherish their wrongs, and let them gnaw like a canker at the heart. Shelley was the only one of the trio named who could appraise criticism at its true worth. Its venom had little vitality in his presence. One passage in Byron's letter is worth quoting both for its references to himself, and to Shelley's drama, *The Cenci*. "I recollect," he says, "the effect on me of the *Edinburgh* on my first poem; it was rage, and resistance, and redress, but not despondency nor despair. I grant that those are not amiable feelings; but, in this world of bustle and broil, and especially in the career of writing, a man should calculate upon his powers of *resistance* before he goes into the arena.

> 'Expect not life from pain nor danger free,
> Nor deem the doom of man reversed for thee.'

"You know my opinion of that *second-hand* school of poetry. You also know my high opinion of your own poetry, because it is of no school. I read *Cenci*, but—besides that I think the *subject* essentially *un*dramatic—I am not an admirer of our old dramatists *as models*. I deny that the English have hitherto had a drama at all. Your *Cenci*, however, was a work of power, and poetry." The reference to the English drama is another instance with the many to prove that Byron was incapable of true literary penetration and criticism. A critic of men, he was but a treacherous guide in literature. It is interesting to note how his better nature was drawn out by his connection with Shelley, though his capacity to be mean and selfish on occasion is unquestionable. Even to his brother poet he behaved shabbily in money matters, and perhaps worse towards his wife. On one occasion he refused to disburse them certain amounts due because no one else refunded, and for no other reason !

Moore appears to have been jealous of Shelley's intimacy with Byron, and he cannot be altogether absolved from the charge of attempting to damage Shelley in the eyes of his brother poet. Moore, of course, was delighted with his *rôle* of guardian to so distinguished a literary lion as Lord Byron ; and the noble poet, whose disposition was of the most easy-going character, gave way but too readily on various occasions to the genial but withal crotchety author of *Lalla Rookh*. The efforts of the minnow, however, to disturb the harmony between the tritons were in vain. Of the uninterrupted friend-liness in the relations between the two great poets there can be no shadow of a doubt, and Byron was powerfully impressed by his friend's death. Moore records that " the melancholy death of poor Shelley seems to have affected Lord Byron's mind with less grief for the actual loss of his friend than with bitter indignation against those who had, through life, so grossly misrepresented him ; and never certainly was there an instance where the supposed absence of all religion in an individual was as-sumed so eagerly as an excuse for the entire absence of truth and charity in judging him." Such, nevertheless, was the actual position of

Shelley towards the world throughout his whole career; those who knew him only by report professed to be horrified and scandalised by his opinions, whilst those who knew him personally, and intimately, almost idolised him.

The friendship of Shelley with another remarkable man—a writer whose singular genius has recently excited renewed interest in the world of letters—deserves more than a casual mention. Thomas Love Peacock became acquainted with Shelley at Great Marlow in the year 1815, and continued to be one of his friends to the end. Peacock left memorials behind him from which many interesting facts are to be gleaned respecting Shelley's literary and other tastes. Considering the weird character of the novels of Charles Brockden Brown, it is not surprising that Shelley was more impressed with that author than with any other whose merits he discussed with Peacock. Constantia Dudley, in Brown's *Ormond*, he held to be one of the highest idealities of female character. As regards the poets, Shakspeare and Milton were read and keenly enjoyed by Shelley, but he did not admire greatly any other of the older poets. Amongst ancient characters, Antigone was the one which most transfixed his imagination. Of the modern poets he devotedly admired Wordsworth and Coleridge. Concerning Wordsworth's stanzas written in a pocket copy of Thomson's *Castle of Indolence*, he said—" It was a remarkable instance of Wordsworth's insight into nature, that he should have made intimate friends of two imaginary characters so essentially dissimilar, and yet generally so true to the actual characters of two friends (Peacock and Shelley), in a poem written long before they were known to each other, and while they were both boys, and totally unknown to him." Shelley had a prejudice against theatres, and on one occasion, seeing the *School for Scandal* performed, he said to Peacock, "I see the purpose of this comedy. It is to associate virtue with bottles and glasses, and villainy with books." Not a totally irrelevant criticism of Sheridan's brilliant play. Shelley was deeply absorbed in Miss O'Neill's performance of Bianca in *Fazio*, and it was evident to Peacock this actress was in his thoughts when he drew the character of Beatrice in the *Cenci*. It was once suggested to Shelley that he should see Miss O'Neill appear in his own drama, but he was almost terrified by the bare contemplation, and emphatically declined, alleging that he could not bear it—a strong tribute to the tragic power of the actress. The opera had more charms for Shelley than the theatre, on ac-

K

count of the music. He especially delighted in
Mozart; went to see *Don Giovanni* and other
operas, but clung more particularly, as his greatest favourite, to *Nozze di Figaro*. A biographer
of the poet, who had no special aptitude for the
work he undertook, and no personal friendship
with Shelley, has gathered together many other personal details; some of these, however, are untrustworthy, and only exaggerated repetitions of more
accurate statements in other quarters. One assertion which this writer makes may be, contradicted
at once, and authoritatively, viz., that Shelley
delighted in shocking people. A single incident of
his life has in this matter led to a wholesale charge.
The poet had far more reason to feel shocked by
the conduct of others than they had by his own.
An instance of this in point. Some one happened
to mention Shelley's name to a respectable tradesman in Great Marlow, when the dry-goods man
became positively alarmed, exclaiming, " Shelley !
why, that is the man who does not believe in the
Devil ! what can become of him ? " The Devil is
essential to the religion of many creeds; but the
tradesman was only carrying out the general
notion entertained of the poet—a notion which, in
this case, had been imbibed from persons who were
supposed to know him much more intimately.

Shelley, all through his existence, suffered from nervous debility, and at one time took laudanum. His absence of mind, too, was in several instances very remarkable; on one occasion, after sitting perfectly silent for a long time, he astonished the company present by quietly asking, "What is the amount of the National Debt?" He also relapsed now and then into a state of lethargy, and once into a condition of somnambulism. All these details only prove the tension at which he lived, and are valuable as side-lights thrown upon this extraordinary being, elucidating much that might otherwise seem inexplicable in his character.

Notwithstanding Peacock's intimacy with Shelley, he failed clearly to understand the poet's nature, and the caricature of him in *Nightmare Abbey*, under the character of Scythrop, is not very happy. There are a few lines of broad farce which sufficiently distinguish the original, but, on the whole, the creation is not so good as many others which Peacock scattered about his novels of men well known in literature. . Shelley himself, however, considered it excellent, and laughed heartily over it, though this kind of literary work was little to his severe taste. We are told that " when Scythrop grew up he was sent, as usual, to a public school, where a little learning was painfully beaten into him, and thence to the University, where it was carefully taken out of him; and he was sent home, like a well-thrashed ear of corn, with nothing in his head; having finished his education to the high satisfaction of the master and fellows of his college, who had, in testimony of their approbation, presented him with a silver fish-slice, on which his name figured at the head of a laudatory inscription in some semi-barbarous dialect of Anglo-Saxonised Latin." This is not a very close parody either of incident or character as relating to Shelley; it fails to distinguish him as those who have studied the man apprehend him; the following passage, which occurs farther on, touches more nearly, in burlesque fashion, the genuine poet, and is considerably more amusing: "At the house of Mr. Hilary, Scythrop first saw the beautiful Miss Emily Girouette. He fell in love; which is nothing new. He was favourably received; which is nothing strange. Mr. Glowry and Mr. Girouette had a meeting on the occasion, and quarrelled about the terms of the bargain; which is neither new nor strange. The lovers were torn asunder, weeping and vowing everlasting constancy; and in three weeks after this tragical event, the lady was led a smiling bride to the altar, by the Hon. Mr. Lackwit; which is neither strange nor new. Scythrop received this intelligence at Nightmare Abbey, and was half distracted on the occasion. It was his first disappointment, and preyed deeply on his sensitive spirit. His father, to comfort him, read him a commentary on Ecclesiastes, which he had himself composed, and which demonstrated incontrovertibly that all is vanity. He insisted particularly on the text, 'One man among a thousand have I found, but a woman amongst all those have I not found.' 'How could he expect it,' said Scythrop, 'when the whole thousand were locked up in his seraglio! His experience is no precedent for a free state of society like that in which we live.'" But those who may be desirous of seeing how much better work of this class Peacock could produce may turn to the caricatures of Coleridge and Byron in the same novel. Unquestionably there were many points of sympathy between Peacock and Shelley. Both were out of harmony with, and indulged a contempt for, the society of their time; but Epicureanism solaced the former, while the latter roamed about the world in a state of semi-distraction, taking things to heart much more deeply than Peacock. The satirist was marvellously enamoured of excellent living; whereas Shelley detested it—lived in the plainest possible manner, and would have rejoiced if he could have dispensed with eating altogether.

Many of Shelley's views upon the conduct and
constitution of society were handled very severely
by Peacock; but both had a common ground in
their love for ancient literature. To both the
Greeks were the apotheosis of humanity. Yet
Peacock detested the ideal in the sense in which
it was almost the life-blood of Shelley, and notwithstanding the friendship that existed between
the two men, there could never be that perfect
understanding, which will ensure such an inter-
pretation of each other's work as to leave no room
for further explanation, and still more loving appreciation.   Great as may justly be our admiration
of Peacock, he is precisely the last man we
should expect to find thoroughly comprehending
such a character as Shelley's.   Therefore, those
who go to Peacock's memorials of Shelley may
reasonably expect to be disappointed either with
the biographer or his subject.   Certain phases of
Shelley's character undoubtedly commended themselves to Peacock, but he was occasionally unjust towards the poet.   There was, manifestly,
much about the life and labours of Shelley
which belonged to a totally different range of
feeling and being from the characteristics which
were so strikingly developed in Peacock and his
inimitable writings.

It was in the year 1818 that Shelley finally expatriated himself from his native land.   He then left England for Italy, never to return.   Weary with his own private griefs, sick with the aspect of public affairs, and afraid—as Lady Shelley has since informed the world—that the Lord Chancellor would deprive him of his infant son by his second wife, he left this country for more clement shores. He made no secret of it, that rather than have his feelings as a parent again outraged, he preferred to abandon England for ever.   Deep as the trial may have been to him personally in some aspects, it undoubtedly had a beneficial effect upon the development of his genius.   The richness of the Italian scenery, the effulgence of the Italian suns, profoundly impressed him, and these have left their mark upon the noble poems which he wrote while travelling from one southern city to another.   Not long, however, was the happiness of Shelley to continue uninterrupted.   In little more than twelve months from the period at which he fled with his child from England, that child was no more.   He died in Rome, and was buried in the English cemetery, Shelley writing in reference thereto—" This spot is the repository of a sacred loss, of which the yearnings of a parent's heart are now prophetic ; he is rendered immortal by love, as his memory is by death. My beloved child lies buried here. I envy death the body far less than the oppressors the minds of those whom they have torn from me. The one can only kill the body; the other crushes the affections." The loss of this son, who was at that time their only surviving child, affected Shelley and his wife most deeply. On Shelley it must have had a peculiarly keen and crushing effect; it seemed as if the very Fates joined with men in endeavouring to prevent the transmission of his name to posterity.

This untoward event drove the poet more and more to the solace of his art; and, as the fruit of some two years of intellectual labour, in 1819-20 appeared two of Shelley's greatest works, *Prometheus Unbound* and *The Cenci*. The climate in which he lived stimulated the brain to a degree which had been quite unparalleled in England, and he wrote his noblest lines with singular ease and freedom.

Shelley's political enthusiasm finds its strongest and most enduring monument in his poems, into which he cast all the energy of his fiery spirit. During his residence in Italy, much occurred in the south of Europe to enlist his warmest sympathies. Liberty, long the dream of ardent patriots, seemed at length to be almost within the range of

universal accomplishment.   After successive re-
volutions in Spain and Naples, Italy began to
stretch her arms about her, desirous of freedom.
The story of that time is well known.   The
struggle of Italy is written in the blood of her
sons; she was crushed by a foreign nation; the
power of Austria was too strong for the first
breathings of the soul of patriotism, and these
breathings were for the time stifled.   So excited
did Shelley become at one period over the struggles
of the Italian people that his usual benevolent
spirit seems almost to have become exorcised, for
we find him writing as follows in the year
1820 :—"At Naples the constitutional party have
declared to the Austrian minister, that if the
Emperor should make war upon them, their first
action would be to put to death all the members
of the Royal Family—a necessary and most just
measure, where the forces of the combatants, as
well as the merits of their respective causes, are so
unequal.   That kings should be everywhere the
hostages for liberty was admirable."   This is an
isolated passage in Shelley's remains upon politics,
and must not blind us to the fact (as there is some
fear of its doing, were it taken alone) that Shelley
was always in favour of proceeding in the accomplishment of his purposes by just and humane

steps.   The fire of freedom which burnt so inex-
tinguishably in his breast received further fuel, not
so much from Italy, however, as from that other
country farther east, whose history has been, perhaps, the most glorious of the human race. Greece,
which has had the honour of stirring with noble
sentiments the minds of more men of genius,
foreign to herself, than any other clime, received
the devotion of Byron, and awoke into the
sublimest transports the soul of Shelley.   Prince
Mavrocordato called on the Shelleys at Pisa, and
informed them that his cousin, Prince Ipsilanti,
had issued a proclamation—that thenceforward
Greece would be free.   This news filled the poet
with the liveliest joy, and he embodied his ex-
ultant feelings in the lyrical drama of *Hellas*,
which was written, he says, " at the suggestion of
the events of the moment, is a mere improvise,
and derives its interest (should it be found to
possess any) solely from the intense sympathy
which the author feels with the cause he would
celebrate."   One needs only to read this drama to
perceive in what school many of our later poets
have studied before attaining their full musical
force and expression.   Take, for example, these
lines from a semi-chorus in Shelley's poem :—

" Through the sunset of hope,
        Like the shapes of a dream,
What paradise islands of glory gleam !
        Beneath Heaven's cope,
        Their shadows more clear float by—
The sound of their oceans, the light of their sky,
The music and fragrance their solitudes breathe,
Burst like morning on dream, or heaven on death,
        Through the walls of our prison ;
        And Greece, which was dead, is arisen ! "

The callous conduct — hypocritical in some
cases—of the European powers generally towards
Greece afflicted Shelley profoundly, and in giving
vent to his righteous indignation in his preface to
Hellas we have a passage bearing a splendid
tribute to that illustrious country. "The apathy
of the rulers of the civilised world," he observes, " to
the astonishing circumstances of the descendants
of that nation to which they owe their civilisation
—rising as it were from the ashes of their ruin,
is something perfectly inexplicable to a mere
spectator of the shows of this mortal scene. We
are all Greeks. Our laws, our literature, our
religion, our arts, have their root in Greece. But
for Greece—Rome, the instructor, the conqueror,
or the metropolis of our ancestors, would have
spread no illumination with her arms, and we
might still have been savages and idolaters; or

what is worse, might have arrived at such a
stagnant and miserable state of social institutions
as China and Japan possess." It is this grand
capacity of going out of himself, and becoming not
only the patriot of his own nation but a citizen
of the world, which makes the poet's song so
deathless, and covers him with a fadeless glory in
the eyes of posterity. Again and again did this
cosmopolitan spirit manifest itself in Shelley. "I
have seen Dante's tomb, and worshipped the sacred
spot," he writes in one letter, and in others gives
full utterance to his reverence for genius and his
passion for liberty.

To follow Shelley through his entire sojourn
in Italy is not my present intention. These
details are to be read elsewhere; but in coming
towards the close of his brief life it is impossible
to avoid reflecting what sorrow the world must
have engraved upon that heart which, before it
throbbed for the last time, caused its owner to
exclaim with melancholy pathos, "If I die to-
morrow, I have lived to be older than my father;
I am ninety years of age." Only twenty-nine is
the real record; and even before these were
attained his hair had become partially white.
Had he avoided the catastrophe which resulted in
his death, there is reason to fear he would not

have passed middle life. A few short years had made strange and rapid changes in him, and on looking back at what he was, he might have exclaimed with Wycherley (though at the close of a different career), when the dramatist gazed in old age upon a portrait representing him in the bloom of youth—" *Quantum mutatus ab illo.*"

I shall not linger over the closing scenes of Shelley's life, but some facts have recently transpired which lend an additional interest to the story of his death. The Shelleys, accompanied by their friends, Lieutenant and Mrs. Williams, left Pisa on the 26th of April 1822 for their new house, the Villa Magni, in the Bay of Spezzia, a point remarkable for its wild and magnificent scenery—the house being on the very border of the sea, with the mountains rising up immediately behind it. A boat was brought from Genoa on the 21st of May, and Shelley and Williams walked to Lerici in order to test her. Williams was enthusiastic over the tiny craft, but it is not a little singular that both Trelawny and Captain Roberts, the builder of the boat, did not think very highly of her. Roberts, it is recorded, had protested, but in vain, against building the boat upon the actual model adopted. Shelley could now experience one of his supremest delights, for boating was to him what swimming

was to Lord Byron.   The former, as we have seen
already, never knew what physical fear was in his
life, and we can therefore imagine the feeling with
which he would regard all exordiums upon the
necessity for careful management.   A large portion
of the coast of Italy was rapidly explored by
Shelley and Williams, and the poet was able to
utilise his voyages for the purposes of his art, as
he invariably kept writing materials on board.
This will account for the extraordinary vigour,
freshness, and first-hand impressions of scenery
discoverable in the verse he wrote at this period.
The *Triumph of Life* was composed as he lay in
his boat, charmed with the beauty and grandeur
of the coast scenery round which the craft continually moved.   A very singular incident is
recorded in the *Shelley Memorials* as having occurred during one of these voyages—it was one
of the few extraordinary visions which the poet
had during his lifetime.   Loud cries being heard
to issue from the saloon, the Williamses wished to
see what was the matter; Mrs. Shelley also
endeavoured to gain the saloon, but fainted outside.
Shelley was discovered in a trance.   On recovering
perfect consciousness, he related that a figure
wrapped in a mantle came to his bedside, and
beckoned him.   He then rose in his sleep, followed

the imaginary figure into the saloon, when it lifted the hood of its mantle, ejaculated "*Siete sodisfatto?*" ("Are you satisfied?") and vanished. The excessive liveliness of the poet's imagination, which was intensified by the themes of his studious contemplation, led him again shortly after this incident to encounter another apparition. This time he was walking with Williams on the beach, when he suddenly pointed to the waves, and exclaimed, "There it is again, there!" His friend states that Shelley declared he saw plainly a naked child (Allegra, who had recently died) rise from the sea, and clasp its hands as if in joy, smiling at him. On the 1st of July 1822, Shelley, accompanied by Williams, left the Villa Magni, to proceed by the boat to Leghorn, with the intention of meeting Leigh Hunt. This journey was accomplished successfully, and Hunt accompanied Shelley to Pisa, where they met Lord Byron, Shelley taking a floor in his lordship's palace, and furnishing it himself. Byron had pledged himself to assist in establishing a magazine which his brother poet was eager to float on behalf of his friend Hunt; but having been persuaded (principally by Moore, who had great influence over him at this period) that it would injure his fame, he now desired to withdraw from his bargain. Lord Byron's be-

haviour on this occasion was one of those exhibitions of the meaner part of his nature which
have detracted from his character.   It affected
Shelley—who believed in the sacredness of obligations—so keenly, that he was almost on the point
of coming to an open rupture with Byron.   Shelley
manifested great depression of spirits when he
left, and this unfortunately proved to be the
last occasion of meeting between these eminent
poets.

Mrs. Shelley appears to have had a strange
presentiment of evil during her husband's absence ;
in fact she had expressed, before he left the Villa
Magni on his expedition, an indefinable dread
which clung to her.   After he had been gone some
time she wrote an urgent letter to him to return,
being still under the influence of " the shadow of
coming misery."   He accordingly hastened his departure from Leghorn, and on July 8th he and
Williams set sail in the *Don Juan* for Lerici.
When they started, black and threatening clouds
were already gathering in the south-west.   Mr.
Trelawny and Captain Roberts witnessed their
departure, and the Genoese mate of the *Bolivar*
remarked to his companion that " the Devil was
brewing mischief."   The rest of that dark day's
work is familiar history.   The day, which had

been intensely hot and oppressive, but profoundly
still, ended with a storm of almost unparalleled
intensity. The elements were speedily lashed
into fury, the thunder roared, and the sea responded
with its still more terrible wave-voices. The
storm, however, as is frequently the case in these
latitudes, was of very brief duration, lasting only
for the space of some twenty minutes. Captain
Roberts had watched the progress of Shelley's
vessel with his glass from the top of the Leghorn
lighthouse; but when the cloud had passed onward,
and Roberts looked again, he "saw every other
vessel sailing on the ocean, except the little
schooner, which had vanished." Now came weary
watching and miserable suspense for Mrs. Shelley.
She and Mrs. Williams imagined that their husbands
might have run the boat ashore and been saved;
and on one of these days of anxiety Lord Byron
was startled by the appearance at Pisa of his
friend's wife rushing into his room, and passionately
demanding to know where her husband was.
Byron gave a graphic picture of this incident afterwards to Lady Blessington. Hope was at length
destroyed by a fearful certainty; and Lady Shelley
thus briefly relates the final knowledge of the
catastrophe; "Two bodies were found on the shore,
one near Via Reggio, the other close to the town

of Migliarino, at the Bocca Lericcio. They lay about four miles apart; Mr. Trelawny went to see both, and recognised the first as the corpse of Shelley, and the second as that of Williams. Williams was nearly undressed, having evidently made an attempt to swim. He had on one of his boots, which Mr. Trelawny recognised by comparing it with another belonging to the same owner. Shelley had probably gone down at once, for he was unable to swim, and had always declared (according to Mr. Trelawny) that in case of wreck he would vanish instantly, and not imperil others in the endeavour to save him."

For many years Shelley's death was believed in England to be attributable to the accidental oversetting of his craft; but this belief has never been shared by his descendants; and the poet's friend who recovered the boat—she was found some two miles away, off the coast of Via Reggio— has stated that the cause of her loss was at once apparent; her starboard quarter was stove in, evidently by a blow from the bows of a felucca; and being undecked, and having three tons and a half of iron ballast, she would have sunk in two minutes. An Italian seaman recently confessed that he was one of those who ran down Shelley's boat, believing that Lord Byron was on board, and that his lordship would pay a heavy ransom for his rescue; and this man stated that the moment the vessel struck, Shelley's craft went down. Several attempts have been made to throw discredit upon this story, for whose accuracy no one could vouch; but as regards the running down, Shelley's relatives have always believed it, though they imagine it was probably the result of a misadventure. Besides the hole discovered in the boat, many circumstances in the attitude of the poet himself confirm the belief that his death was not the result of the accidental oversetting of the boat, but of a collision. Firmly clasped in the hand of Shelley when the boat went down was a copy of Æschylus (not of Keats's poems). Shelley was passionately enamoured of Æschylus, and was apparently reading him at the very moment when the vessel was struck, an occupation which would not have engaged him if the vessel had at that moment been in imminent peril from the storm. There was a volume of Keats in his breast pocket, but the volume of Æschylus, as already intimated, was in his hand, and with the finger clasped in its pages. The volume still opens at the page where Shelley had been reading when the storm arose, and the print of his finger is still to be perceived upon the page. The book was in his hand when the body was found, and it was taken from him by Mr. Trelawny as he laid him on the pile for the burning: the volume remains in the possession of Sir Percy Shelley. The poet had probably, however, been reading Keats's last volume not long before the disaster, for it was found, with some of the pages doubled back, thrust away, probably in haste, into his breast pocket. The copy of Keats had been lent by Leigh Hunt, who told Shelley to keep it till he could give it to him again with his own hands. As the lender would receive it from no one else, it was burnt with the body. Trelawny, speaking of the cremation of Shelley, records a remarkable fact :—" The only portions that were not consumed were some fragments of bones, the jaw and the skull; but what surprised us all was that the heart remained entire." It has been generally stated in biographies of the poet that his ashes were buried in the Protestant cemetery at Rome; but the heart alone reposes in the cemetery—in a space of ground immediately adjoining that where Keats was buried —while the ashes have been preserved at Boscombe Manor, the seat of the Shelley family.

Shelley had wept for "Adonais," had hung upon his words, not very long before that catastrophe which lost to mankind the second poet; and in death, as it were, they were not divided.

Thus perished one of the divinest of English singers, one in memory of whom it was meet and right that Shakspeare's lines should be placed over his grave :—

> " Nothing of him that doth fade,
> But doth suffer a sea change
> Into something rich and strange."

I cannot help recurring to the strange circumstance that the heart of Shelley was indestructible. There was something of him, and that the noblest part, which neither time nor death could conquer or destroy. The impetuous career closed in a tempest from heaven; yet while storm and convulsion presided over the whole of his mortal life, his soul remained calm, and inevitably fixed in love, till the end. The heart which had throbbed so deeply for humanity refused to have even its material substance obliterated. Surviving both flood and fire, it still remained, the symbol of those great and generous feelings which inspired its possessor, emotions entitling him to be regarded as one of the best-beloved spirits of the universe.

It would be difficult to cite a finer tribute to the memory of any man of genius than is to be found in Mrs. Shelley's private journal, written after Shelley's death. A being who could inspire such sentiments in the breast of another must not only have set himself lofty ideals of life, but must in a great measure have attained to the height of those ideals. Mary Wollstonecraft Godwin was no ordinary woman, and yet she compares her own powers and feelings as moonlight to sunlight, when placed beside those of Shelley. Throughout his troubled career, from the first moment they met, she was probably the one individual who alone understood and comprehended the poet, with his manifold desires and schemes for the advancement of humanity. Seeing him, also, as the world never saw him, she has left on record how singularly pure was that soul which had the misfortune to run counter to so many others of human-kind as to earn for itself a heritage of undeserved obloquy. In one passage, addressing the spirit of the departed, she says :—

"You will be with me in all my studies, dearest love! Your voice will no longer applaud me, but in spirit you will visit and encourage me: I know you will. What were I, if I did not believe that you still exist! It is not with you as with another. I believe that we all live hereafter; but you, my only one, were a spirit caged, an elemental being, enshrined in a frail image, now shattered . . . After my William's death, this world seemed only a quicksand, sinking beneath my feet, yet beside me was this bank of refuge—so tempest-worn and frail, that methought its very weakness was strength, and since nature had written destruction on its brow, so the power that rules human affairs had determined, in spite of nature, that it should endure. But that is gone. His voice can no longer be heard; the earth no longer receives the shadow of his form; annihilation has come over the earthly appearance of the most gentle creature that ever yet breathed this air." These reflections are not the rhapsodies of a mind that had lost its balance because of the affliction which had befallen it; the writer possessed one of the strongest and clearest intellects ever bestowed upon a member of her sex. This passionate outcry, also, was the result of a close communion with the spirit of the dead—"I cannot grieve for you, beloved Shelley! I grieve for thy friends—for the world—for thy child—most for myself, enthroned in thy love, growing wiser and better beneath thy gentle influence, taught by you the highest philosophy,—your pupil, friend, lover, wife, mother of your children! The glory of the dream is gone. I am a cloud from which the light of sunset has passed. Give me patience in the present struggle. *Meum cordium cor!* Good night!

'I would give
All that I am, to be as thou now art;
But I am chain'd to time, and cannot thence depart.'"

The theory that a great poet must also be a good prose writer might be supported by references to numbers of instances in both this and other countries. Shelley is an additional proof in favour of the contention. The vigour, clearness, and beauty of his style have seldom been surpassed, though he has not the weighty and stately tread of a Bacon or a Hobbes. Unfortunately for himself, many of the best prose efforts which Shelley has left behind him can only be described as fragments. But even as a fragment, I would point to his *Defence of Poetry* to show what he was capable of achieving in this direction. So far as he has travelled in this argumentative and yet at the same time poetical discourse, he delights us by his power in putting things, and by his extraordinary aptness of illustration. Mrs. Shelley regarded this essay as his only entirely finished prose work, but the feeling after its perusal decidedly is that Shelley intended to supplement it by another paper. Take it as it stands, nevertheless, it is a powerful plea for the divine art in which he excelled, and the various stages of reasoning, enforced in beautiful periods, bear us irresistibly to a conviction of the lofty and dignified vocation of the poet. Reason, he begins by pointing out, is the enumeration of quantities already known, while imagination is the perception of the value of those quantities, both separately and as a whole. This definition of the two forces is very happy, as, also, is the continuation of the thought, that reason is to imagination as the instrument to the agent, as the body to the spirit, as the shadow to the substance. He next proceeds to show how this poetry lies embedded in the heart of man, and is one with him and eternal. Yet all are not singers; only those in whom the faculty of approximation to the beautiful exists to excess are poets,—that is, in the most universal sense of the word. He further brings us to a wide and somewhat startling statement, which at first sight appears to have an ill-grounded basis, but which on closer examination proves how deeply Shelley had studied the question. He remarks that "poets, or those who imagine and express this indestructible order, are not only the authors of language and of music, of the dance, and architecture, and statuary, and painting; they are the institutors of laws and the founders of civil society, and the inventors of the arts of life, and the teachers who draw into a certain propinquity with the beautiful and the true that partial apprehension of the agencies of the invisible world which is called religion. Poets, according to the circumstances of the age and nation in which they appeared, were called, in the earlier epochs of the world, legislators or prophets; a poet essentially comprises and unites both these characters." There is a little vagueness in this statement, for poets are really neither the great artificers nor the actual legislators of the world. They are the instigators of all civilisation, but in many cases the noblest and best poets have failed to do more than simply to indicate. In this sense, therefore, of observers and indicators, they may be said to be the leaders of the world. Their divine moods are the throes from which spring the greatest discoveries. Centuries ago the poet sang of the wondrous beauty that shone in the flowers and grasses of the field, before Linnæus attempted their classification. All the nomenclature and classification which scientific men have given to the forces and products of nature have never once stirred the heart of man; it has been the office of the poet to extract the real secrets of nature, and to read as with an eye of fire her many hidden analogies. We see, then, by this the position which should be assigned to the greatest poet of the world, viz. a loftier and sublimer height than that which we should accord to the greatest exponents of mechanics, science, or philosophy. The philosopher does not necessarily include the poet, though he may, as in the case of Plato and Bacon, in whom poetry certainly dwelt, as Shelley has pointed out; but the great poet always embraces the philosopher, and "Shakspeare, Dante, and Milton are philosophers of the loftiest power." In strains of real eloquence, the essayist, having demonstrated who are poets, proceeds to estimate the effects of poetry upon society. These lines will sufficiently distinguish the scope of his argument, though it is enforced by other passages, till the position he has assumed seems to me impregnable: "The poems of Homer and his contemporaries were the delight of infant Greece; they were the elements of that social system which is the column upon which all succeeding civilisàtion has reposed. Homer embodied the ideal perfection of his age in human character; nor can we doubt that those who read his verses were awakened to an ambition of becoming like to Achilles, Hector, and Ulysses: the truth and beauty of friendship, patriotism, and persevering devotion to an object, were unveiled to their depths in these immortal creations: the sentiments of the auditors must have been refined and enlarged by a sympathy with such great and lovely impersonations, until from admiring they imitated, and from imitation they identified themselves with the objects of their admiration. . . . Ethical science arranges the elements which poetry has created, and propounds schemes, and proposes examples of civil and domestic life: nor is it for want of admirable doctrines that men hate, and despise, and censure, and deceive, and subjugate one another. But poetry acts in another and diviner manner. It awakens and enlarges the mind itself, by rendering it the receptacle of a thousand unapprehended combinations of thought. Poetry lifts the veil from the hidden beauty of the world, and makes familiar objects be as if they were not familiar; it reproduces all that it represents, and the impersonations clothed in its Elysian light stand thenceforward in the minds of those who have once contemplated them as memorials of that gentle and exalted content which extends itself over all thoughts and actions with which it co-exists."

Shelley's devotion to Greek literature was equal to that of Mrs. Browning and other poets of our own time, and it is consequently not surprising to find him assert that "never were blind strength and stubborn form so disciplined and rendered subject to the will of man, or that will less repugnant to the dictates of the beautiful and the true, as during the century which preceded the death of Socrates. Of no other epoch in the history of our species have we records and fragments stamped so visibly with the image of the divinity in man." Much could, of course, be said in deprecation of this as well as other positions assumed by Shelley; to go no further into detail, two ages in the world's history have in sublimity of conception excelled even that of Socrates,—the period of the old Hebrew poets, and our own Elizabethan age. Yet there is a keen pleasure in following Shelley through the remaining stages of this singularly valuable disquisition, which has charmed many men of genius of the present generation. In defending the drama, he regards it as offering the greatest opportunity for effecting the most varied forms of success of any development of the poetic art. Yet occasionally a lack of breadth is perceived in this able dissertation. The great poet has always been a salutary break upon the wheel of progress when a nation has been moving by rapid but disastrous stages. Shelley well observes that "the abolition of personal slavery is the basis of the highest political hope that it can enter into

the mind of man to conceive." While deep in the
treasures of Æschylus, his active sympathies were
in unison with those of Clarkson and Wilberforce.
This expression of opinion on slavery in an elabo-
rately reasoned essay will alone sufficiently demonstrate the vast amount of political and social
enlightenment which had seized upon Shelley's
mind during the later years of his life. He was
on all occasions ready and eager to champion the
claims of woman, for whom he had more than the
ordinary consideration and esteem. He never regarded it as derogatory to the dignity of man to
admit the equality of women. Without insisting
upon it, he also carried conviction of his immense
knowledge and superior originality to the minds
of all with whom he was brought into contact, including that highly-gifted being with whose fortunes his own were united.

Returning for a moment to the *Defence of Poetry*,
—which will be found a remarkable study, even by
those who may be acquainted with more recondite
treatises,—I find this noble passage, in which the
effect upon mankind of the lives of the philosophers is compared with that of the poets : "The
exertions of Locke, Hume, Gibbon, Voltaire,
Rousseau, and their disciples, in favour of oppressed
and deluded humanity, are entitled to the gratitude

of mankind. Yet it is easy to calculate the degree of moral and intellectual improvement which the world would have exhibited had they never lived. A little more nonsense would have been talked for a century or two; and perhaps a few more men, women, and children burnt as heretics. We might not at this moment have been congratulating each other on the abolition of the Inquisition in Spain. But it exceeds all imagination to conceive what would have been the moral condition of the world if neither Dante, Petrarch, Boccaccio, Chaucer, Shakspeare, Calderon, Lord Bacon, nor Milton, had ever existed; if Raphael and Michael Angelo had never been born; if the Hebrew poetry had never been translated; if a revival of the study of Greek literature had never taken place; if no monuments of ancient sculpture had been handed down to us; and if the poetry of the religion of the ancient world had been extinguished together with its belief. The human mind could never, except by the intervention of these excitements, have been awakened to the invention of the grosser sciences, and that application of analytical reasoning to the aberrations of society, which it is now attempted to exalt over the direct expression of the inventive and creative faculty itself." The contemplative mind, which views these questions solely from an unbiassed stand-point, will be much more likely to arrive at the same conclusion as Shelley in regard to the position and influence of poetry upon society and human progress, than it will be ready to adopt a lower estimate. Few there are who will not at once recognise the excellence of the definition that "poetry is the record of the best and happiest moments of the best and happiest minds." Many intuitive and noteworthy things have been said respecting the poetic art, but the one I have just quoted is sufficiently cosmopolitan to touch the sympathies of all, though it may not embrace the perfect fulness of the theme. Take Shelley's treatise as a whole, and rarely has utterance been given to so convincing and eloquent a defence of his race. Though manifestly tinged by the enthusiasm of the writer, this sentiment is not apparent in such a degree as to interfere with sound judgment, or to prevent him from laying down principles which may be useful to the student of the art of poetry.

Captain Medwin published some of Shelley's prose writings in a mutilated form, probably with the best intentions towards his friend, but also with some little lack of discretion. Fortunately, all that the poet left behind him in this respect has now assumed a permanent shape. The influence upon

Shelley's mind of a thorough knowledge of Plato is apparent; no prose author of ancient or modern times had the same power over the poet that he wielded. He drank largely at the fount of his inspiration, and few are acknowledged to have either so thoroughly comprehended the spirit of the original, or so happily to have reproduced it into an alien language. Shelley's translations are remarkable for their flow, melody, and vivacity, and his version of *The Banquet* is a marvel of power and elegance. Unfortunately, other writings which succeeded his efforts in this direction were mostly fragments. Such is the case with two papers on Love and the Coliseum; and with that striking prose idyll known as *The Assassins*. Shelley always had an affection for the weird legend of The Wandering Jew, and we find it occupying a portion of the story forming the basis of the fragment just cited; it is an untoward circumstance that he never had an opportunity of dealing completely with this singular and startling subject. Two other papers by Shelley are of considerable importance as throwing light upon his views on morals. In the *Essay upon Life*, he demonstrates that at one time, at any rate, he was a firm believer in the Immaterial Philosophy of Berkeley. The theory in question, however it may lack accord with the

later tendencies of thought, doubtless gave the
poet many sublime ideas, and permitted him to
revel in that grand and immense exercise of the
imagination which must always have a strange
attraction for a mind constituted like his. With
regard to his views upon religion and immortality,
and the paper upon a future state, lest those who
have done him injustice hitherto should persist in
the same course, it may be as well to refer to what
Mrs. Shelley says respecting his theories. She
distinctly affirms that he certainly regarded the
existence beyond the grave as one by no means
foreign to our interests and hopes. Yet many of
Shelley's biographers have failed to discover in his
writings any clear and unmistakable proof that
he believed in the immortality of the soul. This
is a point of some importance, and traces of such
belief are to be found over and over again in his
works. Mrs. Shelley observes—and her knowledge
is much more trustworthy than the random assertions of inaccurate biographers—that, " considering
his individual mind as a unit, divided from a
mighty whole, to which it was united by restless
sympathies and an eager desire for knowledge, he
assuredly believed that hereafter, as now, he would
form a portion of that whole, and a portion less
imperfect, less suffering, than the shackles insepar-

able from humanity impose on all beneath the moon." Such was Mrs. Shelley's expressed belief; but in Shelley's own words we find such reflections as the following : " The destiny of man can scarcely be so degraded that he was born only to die;" and again, on the occasion of his being in imminent danger at sea—" I had time at that moment to reflect and come to reason on death; it was rather a thing of discomfort and disappointment than terror to me. We should never be separated, but in death we might not know and feel our union as now. I hope, but my hopes are not unmixed with fear for what will befall this inestimable spirit when we appear to die." There is nothing here pointing to annihilation, but strongly to the contrary, in accordance with some previous references I have made to the subject of immortality. In Shelley, of course, there was not the slightest tinge of religious terrorism, and he was precisely the kind of being to defy his Creator if he thought the universe was being conducted upon tyrannical principles; but an intimate knowledge of his character will reveal the presence of an undercurrent of deep religious faith that was never disturbed by the occurrences which agitated his outward life. On many occasions he appeared unconscious of the existence of this sentiment

within himself, but upon others it forced itself
upwards and made utterance, as when he sang :—

" For love, and beauty, and delight,
   There is no death, nor change ; their might
   Exceeds our organs, which endure
   No light, being themselves obscure."

First as a poet, Shelley was yet an acute specu-
lator upon morals. He had a direct and decided
tendency towards metaphysics, but whether he
would have fulfilled all Mrs. Shelley's vaticinations
may be reasonably open to doubt. He had, however, great and unquestionable originality of mind
in this direction. "Had not Shelley deserted
metaphysics for poetry in his youth, and had he
not been lost to us early, so that all his vaster projects were wrecked with him in the waves, he
would have presented the world with a complete
theory of mind, a theory to which Berkeley, Coleridge, and Kant would have contributed ; but more
simple, unimpregnable, and entire, than the
systems of these writers." So observes his most
ardent apologist. It has always been the earnest
belief of philosophers and speculators upon morals,
from the time of Thales to Comte, that their several
systems were the most clear and distinct ever submitted for the approval of mankind ; but the rough
edge of criticism has shown how fallacious have

been these assumptions. We can well afford to
lose one metaphysician more or less in the person
of Shelley the poet; the world prefers his music
to his speculations upon the recondite problems of
human nature.

It frequently occurs that the true poet has
also a true appreciation of, and love for, the kindred
arts of sculpture and painting, though it would be
hazardous to affirm this as a general proposition.
For the details of art, and for particular schools,
the poet may possibly have no special enthusiasm,
but the expression of beauty in any form must
move his soul. The painter also is a poet in the
sense that, when he pursues art from the noblest
motives, it is with a view of elevating men, and
insisting upon the lesson that human life consists
not in the accumulation of material treasure, nor in
the simple enjoyment of material good. Art, as
well as poetry, is humanising in its effects, though
the influence of art is less directly palpable upon
the mind; the sensations produced by it are keen,
but individually evanescent, and its refining influence upon mankind can be perceived in its entirety,
but not in its gradual progress. It moves men
silently and slowly; does not play so great a part
in morals perhaps as music; and certainly not so
operative a part as poetry. Further, the love of

art is a taste which affects the root of the human
character but in a moderate degree, yet it is a taste
which can be encouraged and enkindled in the
commonest minds with substantial success. But
in minds of a superior order it will generally be
found that there is a very strong though sometimes dormant power of appreciation of art. This
power may slumber till the opportuneness of
circumstances calls it into activity. Such was the
case with Shelley. In early years he cared little
for the concrete forms of art, and his first awakening was towards sculpture. Many years elapsed
after that before he expressed any great delight in
painting, but when he did, as we discover in his
Letters from Italy, his sympathy was very strong,
and, upon occasion, penetrating. Correggio and
Guido moved him deeply, the latter, probably,
by reason of the high poetic beauty which generally distinguishes his works. If Shelley erred in
this admiration—as many critics are disposed to
think—he erred in company with thousands who
in every generation have perceived the beauty and
grandeur of Guido's conceptions. Of course, in
matters of art the individual very largely consults
his own taste; it is difficult to lay down canons
and affirm emphatically that they must be accepted. Art affords unbounded scope for em-

piricism. Shelley's aversion to Michael Angelo, during the greater part of his life, should, I think, be chiefly attributed to his horror of materialism. He was touched by the poetry of Guido, but revolted (somewhat unreasonably) from the rougher and more gigantic, but equally sublime, productions of Michael Angelo. Yet, when he knew the latter more intimately, his distaste for him waned. Travel, suffering, and ever-expanding thought enlarged his views; and amongst other prejudices which fell away as the treasures of southern art were unfolded before him in all their beauty, majesty, and sublimity, was his strong feeling of animosity towards the great Italian.

What is of importance to consider here, however, is that the treasures of art, the raptures of music, and the companionship of the illustrious in letters, from Plato downwards, were cherished not alone for the supreme delight which they afforded to the soul of Shelley, but also as incitements to excellence, and ministrants to virtue. Few could bear the light to beat upon their lives, upon their every thought, deed, and emotion, as could this guileless and child-like poet—this man in whom frail humanity and divine genius were combined in a degree at once striking and unique. His life was super-eminently that described in Bailey's *Festus*—

" We live in *deeds*, not years ; in thoughts, not breaths ;
In feelings, not in figures on a dial.
We should count time by *heart-throbs.*   He most lives
Who thinks most ; feels the noblest ; acts the best."

If Shelley never consciously found God, he
drank of the streams of his eternal goodness and
virtue unwittingly; for there is but one Source
whence these streams flow—the universe presents
but one Fountain of benevolence, purity, and love.
After the poet's death, Mrs. Shelley wrote—" To be
something great and good was the precept given
me by my father: Shelley reiterated it."   And
again—" I would endeavour to consider myself a
faint continuation of Shelley's being, and, as far as
possible, the revelation to the earth of what he was.
Yet, to become this, I must change much, and
above all I must acquire that knowledge, and drink
at those fountains of wisdom and virtue from
which he quenched his thirst."   Shelley himself,
in writing to his friend Mr. Hookham (after an
attempt had been made to assassinate the poet in
North Wales), remarked—glad to discover friendship in a world disfigured by deceit and villainy—
" If the discovery of truth be a pleasure of singular purity, how far surpassing is the discovery of
virtue !"   In all seasons, and under all circumstances, he constituted himself the champion of

the oppressed. Nor did he confine his benevolence to pecuniary aid, or the mere language of sympathy. Injustice and suffering evoked in him a personal interest, as in the case of Mr. Finnerty, the Irish patriot, whose imprisonment for libel was referred to in the earlier part of this work. To sustain one whom he regarded as a political martyr, Shelley wrote (in the year 1811) *A Poetical Essay on the Existing State of Things*—a poem whose authorship has latterly excited considerable interest; but which, up to the present moment, remains unfortunately amongst the unrecovered treasures of our literature. And from his earliest years onwards, Shelley never flagged in the prosecution of a practical philanthropy. To the cultivation of virtue and benevolence he devoted himself, not from motives of ostentation or of self-gratulation, but in obedience to those natural instincts which, as we have observed, were in him irresistible from the cradle to the grave. Though he experienced the malevolence of humanity himself, he met inhumanity by humanity, and translated into his daily life the spirit that breathes through the Beatitudes.

Some aspects of Shelley—not so familiar to general readers as the poetic,—that first and greatest which the mention of his name immediately recalls,—have now been presented ; and, upon a close study of his character, it is impossible to understand why the poet should continue to be regarded with the unjust suspicion and unreasonable terror which he excited in so many minds to whom his character can have been but partially known and evolved. His principles of life were few and simple ; and it is not a little singular that many unworthy so-called benefactors of humanity should have been lifted upon the pinnacle of the world's regard, while this man, who never knew what it was to indulge a selfish propensity, only succeeded to an inheritance of misrepresentation and obloquy. That the religious section of society can never be propitiated towards his memory, as prophesied by De Quincey, is incredible under the circumstances of an ever-widening philanthropy of sentiment. Those larger and nobler impulses which are the growing characteristic of English freedom and civilisation, will, in their inevitable march, roll away the opprobrium which has too long attached to the memory of Shelley.

IV.

THE POETRY OF SHELLEY.

> " Art thou not void of guile,
> A lovely soul formed to be blest and bless?
> A well of sealed and secret happiness,
> Whose waters like blithe light and music are,
> Vanquishing dissonance and gloom?   A Star
> Which moves not in the moving Heavens, alone?
> A smile amid dark frowns? a gentle tone
> Amid rude voices? a beloved light?
> A Solitude, a Refuge, a Delight?
> A lute, which those whom love has taught to play
> Make music on, to soothe the roughest day
> And lull fond grief asleep?"
>
> *Epipsychidion.*

IV.

THE POETRY OF SHELLEY.

THAT there is a common and tangible ground for apprehension of the poetic form in thought and language, is proved from the fact that hostile critics, equally with fervent admirers, admit that Shelley was a poet of a true and lofty order. Men are baffled when they endeavour to establish clearly the nature of this subtle poetic essence, but its presence and force in certain writers are universally felt and acknowledged. The most imperfect utterances of Shelley, for example, bear upon them traces of the divine afflatus, and while men will always be divided as to the ultimate value and influence of his works, none will deny that in him originally were those qualities which go to the formation of the Seer. If he failed in the highest branches of his art—and in some aspects there does appear to exist a disparity between his endowments and his poetic creations —we must look for this failure, not in his imaginative and spiritual gifts, but in some intellectual, moral, or physical rift or defect which trammelled or marred his song—sometimes transforming its most hopeful utterances into incoherency, and its native majesty into uncontrolled violence and fury. In Shelley we have to deal with one who pre-eminently—and with God's purpose visibly stamped upon him—was a poet, and yet with one of so mercurial a temperament that his philosophy for the regeneration of the world bore him swiftly along in search of the impracticable. Contradictory in his character, changeful and erratic in his impressions, noble in his sympathies, really sublime when in his highest moods, we find the reflex of all these in his poems. His revolt against society and Christianity dictated *Queen Mab* and kindred effusions; his hatred of oppression found vent in his lines written on the Castlereagh administration, and the political poems of which this is the type; while the rapture and power of his genius only reached their full and perfect enunciation in such works as *The Cenci, Prometheus*, and his magnificent odes. His vision of happiness was unrealisable by others; with all its misery and inequality the world was sufficiently satisfying to their natures, and this depressed him. Then it was he imbibed the idea that animal content under political and religious despotism was due to the so-called teachers, and under the influence of this feeling he was lashed into passion and despair. He held, as he thought, a magician's wand by which he could change earth into paradise; but his incantations were of no avail, and he broke the wand, as Moses broke the tablets, when he perceived the people given over to idolatry. There is much ground to be considered before we rashly condemn Shelley for his defiance of the actual and the real. Probably there is no finer example of devotion to the ideal in literature than he presents for our contemplation; but his excess of spiritual and imaginative vision was aided by no aptitude for the practical, as perceived in Shakspeare and the very greatest poets.

Let us not forget, as one writer has remarked, that Shelley led the existence of a genuine poet. His life was not that of other men's lives. From his earliest years he was wrapt in visions untranslatable by our common vocabulary. He wept in secret, and clenched his hands in anger at the Power which the world said was responsible for the inconsistencies and the jarring elements in all created things. But this spasm of the emotions could not endure for ever. Those who still regard that wild yet singularly beautiful tirade, *Queen*

Mab, as his chief and most admirable work, form a judgment as incomprehensible as it is indefensible ; the Shelley of *Queen Mab* was only a passing phase of a human spirit, a phantom raised speedily to be dispelled. The poet's original notes to that production, wilder in sentiment and more daring in their blasphemy than the poem itself, must perish with it. They are not the final utterances of Shelley upon the high themes which he therein professes to handle, but in reality satirises and defames. We now know that he never intended to publish *Queen Mab* as it appears. Writing to Mr. Ollier, he said :—" In the name of poetry, and as you are a bookseller (you observe the strength of these conjurations), pray give all manner of publicity to my disapprobation of this publication ; in fact, protest for me in an advertisement in the strongest terms." The poet awoke to the conviction that if the buttresses of Christianity were to be undermined it must be by something more potent than invective or slander. At the same time—as I again feel called upon to insist—the poem was not atheistic in the sense in which atheism is generally understood : it is emphatically pantheistic. When he wrote it, the author was an evident disbeliever in a Creative Deity, but he fully accepted the hypothesis of a presiding Spirit permeating all things.

In truth, too much and too little has been made of this poem. It is neither so good nor so bad as continually represented. Its ideas are crude, but in parts its language is singularly flowing and graceful. Its philosophic value may be gauged from the fact that it was projected by Shelley in his eighteenth year and completed in his twentieth —an age quite too early for weighing the universe in the balance, and declaring both man and his Creator to be found wanting.

There is scarcely a page of *Queen Mab* which will not offend, at some point, the moral or religious convictions of the reader; while those passages which have been cited as the finest examples of poetic excellence must appear to the really unprejudiced but as sounding brass and the tinkling cymbal. However gorgeous language may be in itself, it is only valuable as associated with idea; and it is noteworthy that those portions of *Queen Mab* which are most striking in thought are the least ornate in language. The poet, for instance, is much more effective in this passage— though still visionary and impracticable—than he is in numberless other quoted extracts only noticeable for their word-painting :—

"When Reason's voice,
Loud as the voice of nature, shall have waked

N

The nations ; and mankind perceive that vice
Is discord, war, and misery—that virtue
Is peace, and happiness, and harmony ;
When man's maturer nature shall disdain
The playthings of its childhood ;—kingly glare
Will lose its power to dazzle ; its authority
Will silently pass by ; the gorgeous throne
Shall stand unnoticed in the regal hall,
Fast falling to decay ; whilst falsehood's trade
Shall be as hateful and unprofitable
As that of truth is now."

The poet is lucid and forcible when he unveils his republicanism, though his positions may be groundless. If the succeeding passages be distinguished by an underlying fallacy, which causes the poet to flap his wings uselessly against the inevitable, it will be conceded that there is much power in the very structure and essence of the lines :—

" Nature rejects the monarch, not the man ;
  The subject, not the citizen : for kings
  And subjects, mutual foes, for ever play
  A losing game into each other's hands,
  Whose stakes are vice and misery.   The man
  Of virtuous soul commands not, nor obeys.
  Power, like a desolating pestilence,
  Pollutes whate'er it touches ; and obedience,
  Bane of all genius, virtue, freedom, truth,
  Makes slaves of men, and of the human frame
  A mechanised automaton.

" Look on yonder earth :
The golden harvests spring ; the unfailing sun
Sheds light and life ; the fruits, the flowers, the trees
Arise in due succession ; all things speak
Peace, harmony, and love.   The Universe,
In nature's silent eloquence, declares
That all fulfil the works of love and joy,—
All but the outcast, Man.   He fabricates
The sword which stabs his peace ; he cherisheth
The snakes that gnaw his heart ; he raiseth up
The tyrant whose delight is in his woe,
Whose sport is in his agony.   Yon sun,
Lights it the great alone ?   Yon silver beams,
Sleep they less sweetly on the cottage thatch
Than on the dome of kings ?"

Even in his fiercest invective it will be perceived that Shelley cannot suppress his most natural voice, which is not that of the polemic, the
philosopher, or the religious controversialist, but
of the poet.   In the closing lines of the preceding
passages the poetic spirit is really the dominant
element, and this is characteristic of the whole.
If the reader turns to *Queen Mab* as to a literary
curiosity of some value and merit he will not
err ; but if he goes to it for a system of ethics,
and a coherent statement of objections to Christianity, he can only land himself into a quagmire
of bewilderment.   It is the utterance of a soul
disturbed by the echoes of a sceptical philosophy,

but with no power of placing in order and logical
sequence the very premises of that philosophy.

It is essential to be thus plain with regard to
the first work of this distinguished writer, in order
to combat the notion that Shelley is pre-eminently
the poet of *Queen Mab*. If that were the case, our
admiration for him would dissolve as rapidly as
Prospero's vision. It is because of the injustice
done to his memory and position in literature by
accepting this crude and unsatisfactory poem, as
an evidence of the highest exhibition of Shelley's
poetic faculty, that it becomes necessary to dwell
upon it. His belief in " Necessity the mother of
the world," as the only article of his faith, was very
transient, and the less said about this belief perhaps
the better, seeing that it was but the cry of one
groping in the darkness, and not a deliberate conviction arrived at after mental struggles stretching through a number of years. There is, no
doubt, a weird beauty in *Queen Mab* which enchants
the ordinary reader, and gives him a higher appreciation of the poem than a more matured judgment
warrants; but it is the most insubstantial of the
poet's productions, and its creations are vague and
shadowy in the extreme. We move in a land of
golden mist peopled by beings of fantastic shape;
the language we hear has nothing in common with

that spoken by ordinary men; the poet's symbolism passes out of our reach, and his conceptions are altogether superhuman and unrealisable. To frame, therefore, from such hazy material, an indictment against Shelley is sheer injustice—the fabric, as constructed, exists simply for our admiration; the diverse hues of which it is composed are a delight to the senses, but the poem possesses no serious vitality of purpose. As the poet's desire for its suppression could not be, or has not been observed, it remains, what it has indeed been already in part described, a rhapsody—wonderful, it may be, but still a rhapsody —proceeding from one who felt for the first time the flow or motion of the imaginative gift, and whose spirit was a chaos of mingled doubt and emotion.

Shelley afterwards evolved a philosophy, or rather imbibed one by fragmentary processes from various sources. This theory has been most nearly described by the system of idealism, as generally understood. He arrived at the conclusion that thought was universal; nothing existed but "in and through thought." And we here find a solution for the lofty position he constantly assigned to the imagination as a social and operative force in the world, in addition to its functions in the domain of poetry. In his *Essay upon Poetry* he strongly insists that the poet is the greatest regenerator of the world, in that his thought is more refined, and is of a far more exalted kind, than that of any other class of thinkers. The poet is also the collector and interpreter of the thoughts of other men. He holds the crucible from which alone the pure gold can be extracted. " He peoples worlds, and then imagines new." Such was Shelley's theory; but it has been well pointed out by Mr. Masson that, " as is often the case with philosophers, there is a gap in which we cannot see the links connecting Shelley's theoretical or ascending with his practical or descending reason. But he *has* a practical system, and a very definite one. Unlike Hume, he ascends to the extreme of idealism, not to end in indifference or scepticism, but to descend again all the more vehemently upon the world of man and life armed with a faith. He speaks, indeed, of Deity, and other such ideas, as being only 'the modes in which thoughts are combined;' but it is evident, whatever he calls them, that it is only the presence or the absence of certain ideas of this class that constitutes, in his view, the difference between the right and the wrong, between the splendid and the mean in thought. Thoughts combined *so* are eternally noble and good; thoughts combined *otherwise* are eternally ignoble and bad —no man ever cherished a belief of this kind more passionately than Shelley. No man, therefore, had more of the essence of an absolute ethical faith, of a faith not fabricated out of experience, but structurally derived from an authority in the invisible." But when we come to the question how this faith is to be borne into the life of the community generally, we receive no answer. It is to be taught by enthusiasm, and not enforced by reason. This is Shelley's teaching throughout the whole of his poetry. All the evils which oppress humanity are to be abolished by a conformity to some spirit animating nature, but whose likeness has been almost obliterated by the folly and wickedness of mankind. If eternal right and justice could be but perceived by humanity they must henceforth have sway. This was the dream of Shelley, one which he constantly iterated in the ears of men. But, alas for his philosophy! the progress of the world toward the ideal state is not commensurate with the perception of right and justice. Men have long perceived these things, but have their actions conformed to them? The pandemonium of the world is not to be reduced to order by any good or noble thought-combination. Shelley's original hypothesis was wrong. We have seen in the extracts from *Queen Mab*, and they are but an infinitesimal portion of such outpourings, how the poet attributed the numberless evils of the universe to kings, priests, and governments, ignoring

the fact that all these had their origin in the
defective condition of humanity, and are, therefore,
not primarily responsible for its deterioration and
degradation. With the offending institutions swept
off the face of the earth, his vision perceived a
world purged of its guilt and free from its misery.
Yet the changes he desired to effect in the world's
government would exercise little or no influence
towards eradicating the principle of evil. We can
fully admit Shelley's devotion to a liberal and
comprehensive morality, but at the same time
must question the soundness of his theories.

The poem in which Shelley chiefly advocates
these theories of human improvement is *The Revolt
of Islam*, and here we perceive, in its fullest force,
the poet's rebellion against custom and authority.
" Custom," he says, " maketh blind and obdurate
the loftiest hearts ;" and then he unburdens himself
of his anger in the following strain :—

> " Opinion is more frail
> Than yon dim cloud now fading on the moon
> Even while we gaze, though it awhile avail
> To hide the orb of truth : and every throne
> Of Earth or Heaven, though shadow rests thereon,
> One shape of many names :—for this ye plough
> The barren waves of ocean ; hence each one
> Is slave or tyrant ; all betray and bow,
> Command, or kill, or fear, or wreak, or suffer woe.

" This need not be ; ye might arise, and will
 That gold should lose its power, and thrones their
  glory ;
 That love, which none may bind, be free to fill
 The world, like light ; and evil faith, grown hoary
 With crime, be quenched and die. Yon promontory
 Even now eclipses the descending moon !
 Dungeons and palaces are transitory—
 High temples fade like vapour—Man alone
Remains, whose will has power when all beside is gone."

This is not always the poet's mood, however,
through this the longest of his poems. Occasionally there is a gleam of hope and confidence
in the future, and of an active belief in the immortality of goodness and virtue—

" The good and mighty of departed ages
 Are in their graves,—the innocent and free,
 Heroes, and Poets, and prevailing Sages,
 Who leave the vesture of their majesty
 To adorn and clothe this naked world ;—and we
 Are like to them—such perish, but they leave
 All hope, or love, or truth, or liberty,
 Whose forms their mighty spirits could conceive
To be a rule and law to ages that survive.

" Our many thoughts and deeds, our life, and love,
 Our happiness, and all that we have been,
 Immortally must live, and burn, and move
 When we shall be no more."

The Revolt of Islam unquestionably remains an original and striking poem, and in some aspects Shelley's greatest effort. Its invention is marvellous, its imagery abundant to profusion, and the pictures it presents gorgeous in the extreme. Yet, with all this, it is a hopeless and tangled maze to the reader, and must ever continue so. It is imagination run riot—splendid imagination, if you like; but still its licentiousness of fancy is the principal thought remaining in the reader's mind after a perusal of the poem. It is a kaleidoscope, in which the most brilliant colours follow each other in rapid succession, but with no binding zone to encircle the several parts, save that of the hatred of its author for the forms and customs of mankind, and an irrepressible aspiration after liberty. I refrain from discussing the original form of this poem, *Laon and Cythna*, seeing that Shelley was convinced of the propriety of making radical alterations in it. If we cannot commit *Laon and Cythna* to the waters of Lethe, we can, at any rate, leave it to him whom it now only concerns,— the bibliographer. In *The Revolt of Islam* Shelley apostrophises love as the only true governor of the moral world, and is careful to state that when he speaks against the erroneous and degrading idea entertained by some of the Supreme Being, he is not speaking against the Supreme Being himself. In

his preface to the poem, Shelley's abnegation of
atheism is complete, for he expressly says—" The
belief which some superstitious persons whom I
have brought upon the stage entertain of the
Deity, as injurious to the character of his benevolence, is widely different from my own." The
poem is a story of human passion in its broadest
aspects, in which Laon and Cythna, impossible
persons, are mixed up with impossible events in
hopeless perplexity. " It is a succession of
pictures illustrating the growth and progress of
individual mind aspiring after excellence, and
devoted to the love of mankind; its influence in
refining and making pure the most daring and
uncommon impulses of the imagination, the
understanding, and the senses; its impatience at
' all the oppressions that are done under the sun;'
its tendency to awaken public hope, and to en-
lighten and improve mankind; the rapid effects
of the application of that tendency; the awakening
of an immense nation from their slavery and
degradation to a true sense of moral dignity and
freedom; the bloodless dethronement of their
oppressors, and the unveiling of the religious
frauds by which they had been deluded into sub-
mission; the tranquillity of successful patriotism,
and the universal toleration and benevolence of

true philanthropy; the treachery and barbarity of hired soldiers; vice not the object of punishment and hatred, but kindness and pity; the faithlessness of tyrants; the confederacy of the Rulers of the World, and the restoration of the expelled Dynasty by foreign arms; the massacre and the extermination of the Patriots, and the victory of established power; the consequences of legitimate despotism—civil war, famine, plague, superstition, and an utter extinction of the domestic affections; the judicial murder of the advocates of Liberty; the temporary triumph of oppression, that secure earnest of its final and inevitable fall; the transient nature of ignorance and error, and the eternity of genius and error." Such are the pictures, as Shelley himself intimates, by which he intended to inculcate his views of man and society in this poem; his nature at the time of its production having been stirred to its depths by the French Revolution and subsequent events. But with persons as impalpable as the dagger of Macbeth, and incidents so intricate and inconsequent that it is impossible to trace their course, it is not greatly to be wondered at that the poem should fail to strike deep root. The probability is that the readers and admirers of this poem could be numbered upon one's fingers; yet Shelley's imagina-

tion was never displayed to greater advantage than
where it revels in isolated passages of this narrative,
describing the journeyings of Laon and Cythna.
To demonstrate Shelley's command of felicitous
imagery, and to show his power of delineating
true and minute pictures upon an incredibly small
piece of canvas, take these two stanzas :—

" The blasts of Autumn drive the winged seeds
    Over the earth,—next come the snows, and rain,
    And frosts, and storms, which dreary Winter leads
    Out of his Scythian cave, a savage train ;
    Behold ! Spring sweeps over the world again,
    Shedding soft dews from her ethereal wings ;
    Flowers on the mountains, fruits over the plain,
    And music on the waves and woods she flings,
And love on all that lives, and calm on lifeless things.

" O Spring ! of hope, and love, and youth, and gladness,
    Wind-winged emblem ! brightest, best, and fairest !
    Whence comest thou, when with dark Winter's sadness
    The tears that fade in sunny smiles thou sharest ?   .
    Sister of joy ! thou art the child who wearest
    Thy mother's dying smile, tender and sweet ;
    Thy mother, Autumn, for whose grave thou bearest
    Fresh flowers, and beams like flowers, with gentle feet,
Disturbing not the leaves which are her winding-sheet."

The following stanza, allegorically describing
the world under the season of Winter, which must
be displaced to make way for the new birth of
Spring,—concludes with a magnificent image :—

" This is the Winter of the world ;—and here
  We die, even as the winds of Autumn fade,
  Expiring in the frore and foggy air.—
  Behold ! Spring comes, though we must pass, who made
  The promise of its birth,—even as the shade
  Which from our death, as from a mountain, flings
  The future, a broad sunrise ; thus arrayed
  As with the plumes of over-shadowing wings,
From its dark gulf of chains, Earth like an eagle springs."

Although only two years elapsed between the production of *Queen Mab* and *Alastor*, the latter poem exhibits a marked advance in the poetic art. It is worthy of Shelley in his best period. Devoid of what I may call the sensational elements which disfigure *Queen Mab*, it is rounded and complete, and charged with beauty and deep reflection. In two short years the poet had been taught the hopelessness of the campaign against error—upon which he had entered with so much enthusiasm— and though he had not abandoned his opinions, it is obvious that a marked change had come over the writer of these two works. *Alastor* is imbued with a grand and touching melancholy. We behold the student who has drank deeply at every accessible spring of knowledge and finds his thirst still unappeased. For some time he contemplates the Infinite with satisfaction, having dismissed from his conceptions material things, but an ever-

burning and increasing desire gnaws at his heart—
he longs for something, he knows not what. He con-
ceives an ideal being, upon whom he centres every
perfection, ransacking the ages to add to the glory
which gathers round her. But where is such a
being? Disappointed in his quest, Alastor is represented as despairing of ever finding this perfect
image, and in consequence he is overtaken by a
premature death. In the outset of his career

> " The fountains of divine philosophy.
>   Fled not his thirsting lips ; and all of great,
>   Or good, or lovely, which the sacred past
>   In truth or fable consecrates, he felt
>   And knew. When early youth had past, he left
>   His cold fireside and alienated home,
>   To seek strange truth in undiscovered lands."

He lingered in Athens, Jerusalem, and Babylon,
wandered through Arabia, Persia, and India, till,
in the Vale of Cachmire, came to him the conception of a perfect being, whose voice was as the
voice of his own soul. Their spirits met together ;
but his trance is quickly over, the vision has departed, and Alastor once more begins the weary
quest of his ideal. Sleep and death divide them,
and he wastes in despair, but still travels on. All
labour is vain, and Alastor is left to death and the
grave. This is the end and sum of all things :—

"Art and eloquence,
And all the shows o' the world, are frail and vain
To weep a loss that turns their light to shade.
It is a woe 'too deep for tears,' when all
Is reft at once, when some surpassing Spirit,
Whose light adorned the world around it, leaves
Those who remain behind nor sobs nor groans,
The passionate tumult of a clinging hope ;
But pale despair and cold tranquillity,
Nature's vast frame, the web of human things,
Birth and the grave, that are not as they were."

The whole of this poem is noble; it is characterised by a pure and solemn spirit, and its evident
allegory is not without its purport for mankind.
On the one hand we have the up-welling joy and
happiness which fill the student, as life and nature
unfold to him their mysteries, and on the other
is graphically delineated the burden of sorrow for
all created things, that they contain not in their
most secret places and recesses that ideal perfection which the mind can conceive but is unable
to grasp.   There is also enfolded a second meaning
in *Alastor* for those whom the poet describes as
"morally dead."   Those who have no hopes, no
joys or sorrows in common with humanity, who
have no desires after the pure and the exalted in
sentiment and being, Shelley maintains "are
neither friends, nor lovers, nor fathers, nor citizens

of the world, nor benefactors of their c
Among those who attempt to exist without sympathy, the pure and tender-hearted perish through the intensity and passion of their search after its communities, when the vacancy of their spirit suddenly makes itself felt. Those who love not their fellow-beings live unfruitful lives, and prepare for their old age a miserable grave." Such are some of the higher teachings of *Alastor*, a work which, if not so great as the *Prometheus Unbound*, is one of the most extraordinary which Shelley has bequeathed to us.

An electric dazzle plays round all the poetry of this writer. His sensibility is so keen that he appears to be constantly under the influence of a galvanic battery, which strains his nerves to the highest tension. Of an order which, as we saw at the outset, is the very antithesis of that of Pope, he is yet more fervid than any other of the imaginative school. His imagery is ceaseless and inexhaustible. In beauty of expression merely, probably no poet of either ancient or modern times has equalled even, much less transcended him; and it is only when we come to the more substantial attributes of the great poet that we are sensible of his defects. Yet, looking at what he has accomplished, Macaulay considered himself justified in pronouncing upon him a fervid eulogy, with which the coldest critic of Shelley cannot but largely agree.

Referring to the great imaginative gifts of Bunyan, the essayist observed that in this respect the genius of the author of *The Pilgrim's Progress* "bore a great resemblance to that of a man who had very little else in common with him, Percy Bysshe Shelley. The strong imagination of Shelley made him an idolater in his own despite. Out of the most indefinite terms of a hard, cold, dark, metaphysical system, he made a gorgeous Pantheon, full of beautiful, majestic, and life-like forms. He turned atheism itself into a mythology, rich with visions as glorious as the gods that live in the marble of Phidias, or the virgin saints that smile on us from the canvas of Murillo. The Spirit of Beauty, the Principle of Good, the Principle of Evil, when he treated of them, ceased to be abstractions. They took shape and colour. They were no longer mere words, but 'intelligible forms,' 'fair humanities;' objects of love, of adoration, or of fear. As there can be no stronger sign of a mind destitute of the poetical faculty than that tendency which was so common among the writers of the French school to turn images into abstractions—Venus, for example, into Love, Minerva into Wisdom, Mars into War, and Bacchus into

Festivity, so there can be no stronger sign of a
mind truly poetical than a disposition to reverse
this abstracting process, and to make individualities
out of generalities. Some of the metaphysical and
ethical theories of Shelley were certainly most
absurd and pernicious. But we doubt whether
any modern poet has possessed in an equal degree
some of the highest qualities of the great ancient
masters. The words bard and inspiration, which
seem so cold and affected when applied to other
modern writers, have a perfect propriety when applied to him. He was not an author, but a bard.
His poetry seems not to have been an art, but an inspiration. Had he lived to the full age of man, he
might not improbably have given to the world
some great work, of the very highest rank in design
and execution." Substantially, as I have said, all
must endorse this estimate; but the question of
Shelley's poetry by no means ends here. His
admirers have been too fervid in their admiration,
—or so, at least, it has been affirmed,—and his detractors too depreciatory in their detraction. In the
midst of truly wonderful work, Shelley has written
occasionally inflated poetry, which has no kind of
relevance to "things in heaven, or things in earth,
or things under the earth." Nevertheless, with here
and there defective and discordant notes, his mind

had yet a great and noble tone : and they wrong
his memory most who unhesitatingly describe as
perfect and sublime, work which, in maturer years,
the poet himself would have described as shallow
and inferior. It is his unbounded luxuriance of
imagery which incapacitates many from perceiving
the want of depth in some of his utterances, and
his constant brilliancy deprives for the moment
such admirers of their natural vision. The most
transient feelings may · be expressed with such
perfect music that the senses shall be charmed and
the intellect laid to sleep ; and unquestionably this
is the influence which some portion of Shelley's
writings is calculated to produce. Wisdom and
reason go to the making of the greatest poets, as
well as that mystical enchantment which proceeds
from the thrilling tones of the lyre. It is because
Shelley so truly reads nature in *Alastor*, and gives
us careful and penetrating observation as well as
the hidden harmony of verse, that it takes an
infinitely higher rank than poems of the type of
Queen Mab. Shelley is always beautiful in diction ;
yet beauty, without thought, is but the shadow
and semblance of poetry, and not the living,
breathing form itself. Thought must, after all, be
the innate force of poetry—her soul—her vitality ;
music and imagery but the robes wherewith she is

clothed. It is in the combination of the three that we look for the justly great poet.

In the preface to his drama of *Philip van Artevelde*, Sir Henry Taylor—briefly discussing the poetry of Lord Byron and of Shelley—takes the opportunity of pointing out that the maxim describing the poet as " of imagination all compact " should not be adopted too literally. The advice is not altogether unnecessary, for there is some danger still of the fancy and the imagination being unduly regarded as the only essentials to successful and durable poetry. We are reminded that imagination and passion may, unsupported, make a rhapsodist, or a visionary, but nothing more. Reflection and observation must play no unimportant part in the constitution of the poet. Upon what are his divine powers to be fed, if these are neglected ? An uninformed and unobservant poet may make melody to please the ear, but he will never nourish the soul. In proportion as Shelley advances from the melodious singer, and nothing more, towards the full-orbed poet, in that proportion does he become great. Instead of phantoms he then creates individuals, as in *The Cenci;* instead of meaningless melody we get true music, as in his *Adonais* and magnificent lyrics. The highest poetry, then, is not the outcome of the musical talent alone;

delightful sounds are nothing if unaccompanied by
that spiritual lesson it is the office of the poet to
express, or that hidden meaning which it belongs
to the Seer to expound. There is more of real
poetry and immortal essence in one true lyric than
in a purposeless, vague, and yet verbally perfect
epic. When a poet has passed out of the stage of
mere rhetorical music, and has communed with
man and nature in the sense described by Wordsworth, we may fairly look for those riper fruits
which such experience is calculated to produce.
It is then that he rises to the sublimest height of
his art. His perceptions have become keener and
truer, and he can say, with the last-named great
singer of his race,—

> " I have learned
> To look on Nature, not as in the hour
> Of thoughtless youth ; but hearing oftentimes
> The still, sad music of humanity,
> Not harsh nor grating, though of ample power
> To chasten and subdue. And I have felt
> A presence that disturbs me with the joy
> Of elevated thoughts : a sense sublime
> Of something far more deeply interfused,
> Whose dwelling is the light of setting suns,
> And the round ocean, and the living air,
> And the blue sky, and in the mind of man,
> A motion and a spirit that impels
> All thinking things, all objects of all thought,
> And rolls through all things."

The true speech of the poet, the articulate voice begotten of such observation as Wordsworth here depicts, has been well distinguished by Emerson— "We are symbols and inhabit symbols: workmen, work, and tools, words and things, birth and death, all are emblems; but we sympathise with the symbols, and being infatuated with the economical uses of things we do not know that they are thoughts. The poet, by an ulterior intellectual perception, gives them a power which makes their old use forgotten, and puts eyes and a tongue into every dumb and inanimate object. He perceives the independence of the thought in the symbol,—the stability of the thought, the accidency and fugacity of the symbol. As the eyes of Lynceus were said to see through the earth, so the poet turns the world to glass, and shows us all things in their right series and procession. For, through that better perception he stands one step nearer to things, and sees the flowing or metamorphosis; perceives that thought is multiform; that within the form of every creature is a force impelling it to ascend into a higher form; and, following with his eyes the life, uses the forms which express that life, and so his speech flows with the flowing of nature. All the facts of the animal economy, sex, nutriment, gestation, birth, growth, are symbols of the passage of the world into the soul of man, to suffer there a change, and reappear a new and higher fact. He uses forms according to the life and not according to the form. This is true science. The poet alone knows astronomy, chemistry, vegetation, and animation, for he does not stop at these facts but employs them as signs. He knows why the plain or meadow of space was strewn with these flowers we call suns, and moons, and stars; why the great deep is adorned with animals, with men, and gods; for in every word he speaks he rides on them as the horses of thought. By virtue of this science the poet is the Namer or Language-maker." He is the link between God and man. The delegate of the Creator, he speaks his language to the creature. He is, emphatically, the voice of God.

We thus perceive that the poet, while not in our presence begetting any sense of inferiority in us, is immeasurably our superior when surveying man and nature in his contemplative mood. He perceives analogies which would pass unnoticed by ordinary men—he establishes relations between objects which we deemed to lie irreparably asunder —he finds in the seasons a corresponding life to that of humanity, and he unveils the very heart and meaning of created things.

In his later years Shelley was ripening into

such a poet. The reed upon which he played
with such marvellous musical skill began to be
distinguished for the deeper undertones of thought.
He was rapidly qualifying, when death so treacher-
ously overtook him, to take his place amongst the
great Seers of mankind. His griefs were becoming
sublimated to the highest uses, and his nature
was being quickly purged of its dross. Even
when he wrote *Julian and Maddalo* he had begun
to create as well as to sing. The characters in
this poem assume the ordinary shapes of humanity
—and these autobiographical sketches may be
readily apprehended and understood by the general
reader. The narrative was intended by Shelley to
be a translation of poetic thought into familiar
language, with himself and Byron as the speakers.
It is a representation of the real and not the ideal,
and, as such, is successful from the artistic point of
view. The poem is valuable—if for no other reason
—as showing the new life dawning upon Shelley,
with its influence upon his poetry. The element
of the practical, as touching the right use of his
divine gift—which seemed previously as far from
his grasp as the noon-day sun—is brought near in
this record of the story of the madman in San
Lazzaro, at Venice. Moreover, the characteristics
of Maddalo and Julian—the pride and ambition

of the former, the philosophy and heterodoxy of
the latter—are well distinguished. We now recognise, in short, some affinity between Shelley
and the rest of the human species.

The highest achievement of Shelley in ideal
poetry is the *Prometheus Unbound*, frequently
regarded now as perhaps the greatest of all his
works. Saturated with the sublime tragedies of
Æschylus, the modern poet conceived the idea of
completing three dramas after the Greek type.
Two of these—one founded upon the story of Tasso,
and the other upon the Book of Job—were never
undertaken. The third only remains to us.
Æschylus among the literary gods and demigods
had an irresistible attraction for Shelley, and his
own conceptions at length found vent in this
remarkable lyric drama. The work is not without
its interest for every person, apart from its poetry,
by its symbolism, and the use Shelley has made
of mythology. A great moral purpose runs through
the drama, whose principal features remain vividly
impressed upon us. Prometheus, chained to the
rock by Jupiter, represents the whole race of
humanity suffering under the sway of evil. Asia
represents nature, and when evil is overthrown,
she is espoused by Prometheus, now delivered
from his chains—the poet thereby intending to

show the ultimate triumph of good. Prometheus is regarded by Shelley as a higher being than the Satan of Milton and the generally-conceived character of the Prince of Darkness. He is considered to be the type of the highest perfection of moral and intellectual nature, impelled by the purest and the truest motives to the best and noblest ends. In addition to the heroic attributes usually ascribed to Satan—courage, majesty, and endurance—Prometheus is portrayed as a being of too lofty a nature to indulge in the passions of envy, revenge, and the thirst for self-aggrandisement. Shelley departed from the ancient fable in one important respect—he represents Prometheus as refusing to yield to the oppressor of mankind, whereas in the lost drama of Æschylus there is supposed the reconciliation of Jupiter with his victim as the price of the disclosure of the danger threatened to his empire by the consummation of his marriage with Thetis. In whatever light we view Shelley's drama it is a remarkable production. It is grand and magnificent in scope; its moral purport is lofty; the passions of its persons are the passions of superhuman creations; the whole subject is steeped in the most gorgeous colours of which poetry is capable; while its music is more splendid and sonorous than anything which had hitherto proceeded from the golden mouth of the singer. Always daring, frequently to rashness, in his speculations, Shelley has here transcended every other example of this quality of his mind—he has thrown off all trammels, and given us, through the vivid medium of his allegory, his idea of man, free and erect before the Spirit of all things, and triumphant after ages of suffering. It is a grand conception, and the artistic skill with which the poet has woven out his ideas is worthy of the conception. A higher eulogy than that could scarcely be passed upon this or any similar enterprise. Its rank in the scale of great imaginative works is, of course, beneath the inspirations of Dante and those few spirits of the same sublime calibre, but only beneath these—to no inferior level can it be relegated.

In the first act of the drama are many passages of which the following, with its passionate energy, may be taken as a fair type. It occurs in the closing part of the dialogue between Prometheus, Panthea, and the Fury, and is a picture of the confusion that has come upon all things :—

" *Fury.* Blood thou canst see, and fire ; and canst hear
    groans :
Worse things unheard, unseen, remain behind.
    Prometheus. Worse ?

Fury.   In each human heart terror survives
The ravin it has gorged : the loftiest fear
All that they would disdain to think were true :
Hypocrisy and custom make their minds
The fanes of many a worship, now outworn.
They dare not devise good for man's estate,
And yet they know not that they do not dare.
The good want power, but to weep barren tears.
The powerful goodness want : worse need for them.
The wise want love; and those who love want wisdom ;
And all best things are thus confused to ill.
Many are strong and rich, and would be just,
But live among their suffering fellow men
As if none felt : they know not what they do.
  Prometheus. Thy words are like a cloud of winged snakes ;
And yet I pity those they torture not.
  Fury. Thou pitiest them ? I speak no more ! [*Vanishes.*
  Prometheus.   Ah, woe !
Ah, woe ! Alas ! pain, pain, ever, for ever !
I close my tearless eyes, but see more clear
Thy works within my woe-illumined mind,
Thou subtle tyrant ! Peace is in the grave.
The grave hides all things beautiful and good :
I am a God, and cannot find it there,
Nor would I seek it ; for, though dread revenge,
This is defeat, fierce king ! not victory.
The sights with which thou torturest gird my soul
With new endurance, till the hour arrives
When they shall be no types of things which are.
  Panthea. Alas ! what sawest thou ?
  Prometheus.   There are two woes ;
To speak, and to behold :—thou spare me one.

Names are there, Nature's sacred watchwords, they
Were borne aloft in bright emblazonry;
The nations thronged around, and cried aloud,
As with one voice, Truth, Liberty, and Love !
Suddenly fierce confusion fell from heaven
Among them : there was strife, deceit, and fear :
Tyrants rushed in, and did divide the spoil.
This was the shadow of the truth I saw."

Although this drama is and ever has been a source of considerable perplexity, yet by a careful process of disintegration the reader will be able to get at the moral truths Shelley is desirous of enforcing. Sometimes, however, darkness ensues from excess of light, and the poetic ideal so predominates in *Prometheus* as almost to blind us to whatever additional claims it may have upon us. The choruses absolutely ring with music, and the speeches in blank verse teem with imagery. I have given a specimen of Shelley's power and energy in this drama; let me now quote a passage for its extraordinary beauty of language and imagery. The scene depicted is morning in a lonely vale of the Indian Caucasus, where Asia is waiting for her sister Panthea :—

" *Asia.* From all the blasts of heaven thou hast
        descended :
Yes, like a spirit, like a thought, which makes
Unwonted tears throng to the horny eyes,

And beatings haunt the desolated heart,
Which should have learnt repose : thou hast descended,
Cradled in tempests ; thou dost wake, O Spring !
O child of many winds ! As suddenly
Thou comest as the memory of a dream,
Which now is sad because it hath been sweet ;
Like genius, or like joy, which riseth up
As from the earth, clothing with golden clouds
The desert of our life.—
This is the season, this the day, the hour ;
At sunrise thou shouldst come, sweet sister mine,
Too-long desired, too-long delaying, come !
How like death-worms the wingless moments crawl !
The point of one white star is quivering still
Deep in the orange light of widening morn
Beyond the purple mountains : through a chasm
Of wind-divided mist the darker lake
Reflects it ; now it wanes : it gleams again
As the waves fade, and as the burning threads
Of woven cloud unravel in pale air :
'Tis lost ! and through yon peaks of cloud-like snow
The roseate sun-light quivers : hear I not
The Æolian music of her sea-green plumes
Winnowing the crimson dawn?

[PANTHEA *enters.*
I feel, I see
Those eyes which burn through smiles that fade in tears,
Like stars half-quenched in mists of silver dew.
Belovèd and most beautiful, who wearest
The shadow of that soul by which I live,
How late thou art ! the spherèd sun had climbed
The sea ; my heart was sick with hope, before
The printless air felt thy belated plumes."

The speech in which Asia details the creation
of the world and of man is very powerful; yet
the lyric portions of the drama are probably those
which will remain most deeply rooted in popular
favour.   The fourth act is a marvellous triumph of
melody from its opening to its closing lines.   What
poet has in this respect excelled these stanzas,
which are a fitting introduction to the last stage
of this lyrical drama ?—

> "VOICE OF UNSEEN SPIRITS.
>
> " The pale stars are gone,
>   For the sun, their swift shepherd,
>   To their folds them compelling,
>   In the depths of the dawn,
> Hastes, in meteor-eclipsing array, and they flee
>   Beyond his blue dwelling,
>   As fawns flee the leopard,
>   But where are ye ?

> "*A train of dark Forms and Shadows passes by confusedly*
> *singing.*

> " Here, oh ! here :
>   We bear the bier
> Of the Father of many a cancelled year !
>   Spectres we
>   Of the dead Hours be,
> We bear Time to his tomb in eternity.

" Strew, oh strew !
Hair, not yew !
Wet the dusty pall with tears, not dew !
Be the faded flowers
Of Death's bare bowers
Spread on the corpse of the King of Hours !
Haste, oh haste !
As shades are chased,
Trembling, by day, from heaven's blue waste.
We melt away,
Like dissolving spray,
From the children of a diviner day,
With the lullaby
Of winds .that die
On the bosom of their own harmony !"

The choruses of Spirits of the Mind are all equal
to this in ease and lilt of rhythm, as well as in
that power of haunting the memory when the
last cadence has died away, which is so peculiar
a characteristic of the lyrics of Shelley. In the
whole poem a strength and a majesty are percep-
tible, which were only indicated, never fully displayed, in previous conceptions.

It is matter for regret that Shelley did not
more frequently woo those moods in which his
own soul might find distinct points of contact and
sympathy with the rest of mankind. Mrs. Shelley
was desirous that he should adopt subjects more
adapted to the popular taste and apprehension

P

than the dreamy and abstract which had for him the greatest charm. The consequence is, that while the world has much over which it can rejoice as the produce of his genius, a finer harvest has been lost to it. Look, for instance, at *The Witch of Atlas*, another poem of the ideal school, and one absolutely prodigal in fancy. This is one of the most Shelleyan of all Shelley's poems, for the freedom with which the reins are given to the imagination. He has allowed the steeds yoked to the fiery car of Fancy to bear him whither they will, and it is beyond the power of others to follow him in his career. Consequently, however beautiful *The Witch of Atlas* may be as a triumph of the fancy, men will be tempted to ask concerning it, *Cui bono?* Although art may not always involve simplicity of purpose, there is a point at which hopeless confusion and an obvious lack of purpose forbid us to associate art with anything in which these are conjoined; unless, indeed, an artist or a poet be satisfied that mere colour and musical sound are art, in which case we should be compelled to assign a high position to *The Witch of Atlas*. But the popular judgment and instinct in this matter are right. Similar reflections arise upon reading *Epipsychidion*, of which Shelley himself observed that few would fitly conceive its reasoning. He calculated that there were not one hundred persons capable of judging and feeling rightly with respect to a composition of so abstruse a nature. Yet a great deal of poetic treasure is embedded in it—enough to have sufficed for half-a-dozen poems with practical aims and objects. The poet delighted to revel in fanciful mazes, whither his fellow-men could not advance, and in *Epipsychidion* he enjoyed the distinction of having fabricated a Gordian knot which none of his admirers and commentators has been able to unravel. Such an enterprise, however pleasant, and however splendidly executed, only serves to divorce the poet from that position of teacher and prophet of humanity to which it should be his most ardent hope to aspire. The circumstances under which this poem were produced were very romantic, and it appears chiefly to be a panegyric of love, founded on Shelley's feelings towards an Italian lady. It is perhaps needless to say that these feelings bore no tinge of any other character save the Platonic. Shelley was so constituted, and so worshipped goodness, beauty, and virtue, that he was capable of being inspired by truly Platonic sentiments. This is how the poem should probably be read, but, in truth, here again we are met by one

of that series of poems which afford only psycho-
logical problems wrapped in the most beautiful
poetic forms.

In *Adonais* and *Hellas*, fortunately, we obtain
more foothold. The former takes rank after the
finest of elegiac poems, the *Lycidas* of Milton, and
might have been counted worthy of equality with
it had Shelley been Milton's predecessor. If it
be the first quality of the elegiac poem to fix the
grief of the singer upon the heart and mind of the
listener, Shelley's poem fulfils this requirement.
When once read, it is ever remembered, and the
echo of the opening lines clings to the memory in
the midst of the absorption of ever-varying ideas.
The popular belief that Keats had died of an over-
dose of criticism no doubt plunged Shelley's soul
into a paroxysm of grief and anger—hence the
depth and sincerity of the poem. We now know
that Keats was not "snuffed out by an article;"
but Shelley's noble expression of regret still retains
its place with us, and will continue to do so.
Few passages in modern writers equal that describing the awakening of the Earth after winter, and
the setting forth by contrast of the non-awakening
of the poet; but the whole is extremely beautiful,
luxuriant, and tender in its grief, and studded with
rich gems of imagery.

With such a theme as Greece, and her struggles for freedom, it was to be expected that Shelley would rise to the full height of his inspiration. The adulation of the Greeks in his preface to *Hellas* seems almost extravagant, notwithstanding that the race has occupied the highest pinnacle of fame in the world's history. But men ever pardon excess in a noble cause. At the time of the composition of the lyrical drama of *Hellas*, Shelley was regarding with the deepest interest the struggles in Spain and Italy, which it is said he looked upon as "decisive of the destinies of the world, probably for centuries to come." While these struggles were in progress, a revolution broke out in Greece, and the poet hailed the new effort after freedom with the wildest enthusiasm. Under the influence of this feeling he produced *Hellas*, but as the war at the time had not concluded, he was compelled to give a vague and shadowy termination to his drama. It remains one of the most perfect of his productions, if we bear in mind the quality of its music alone. In construction—principally through the element of uncertainty which was necessarily connected with it—Shelley regarded it as faulty. It is in this drama, however, that he touched the highest point of lyrical excellence. No work of his, nor indeed of any other modern poet, gives us

stanzas superior to these, for their vivid imagination
and picturesque force :—

> " Worlds on worlds are rolling ever
>   From creation to decay,
> Like the bubbles on a river,
>   Sparkling, bursting, borne away.
>   But they are still immortal
>   Who, through birth's orient portal,
> And death's dark chasm hurrying to and fro,
>   Clothe their unceasing flight
>   In the brief dust and light
> Gathered around their chariots as they go ;
>   New shapes they still may weave,
>   New gods, new laws receive,
> Bright or dim are they, as the robes they last
>   On Death's bare ribs had cast.
>
> A Power from the unknown God,
>   A Promethean conqueror came ;
> Like a triumphal path he trod
>   The thorns of death and shame.
>   A mortal shape to him
>   Was like the vapour dim
> Which the orient planet animates with light ;
>   Hell, Sin, and Slavery came,
>   Like blood-hounds mild and tame,
> Nor preyed until their lord had taken flight.
>   The moon of Mahomet
>   Arose, and it shall set :
> While, blazoned as on Heaven's immortal noon,
>   The Cross leads generations on.

Swift as the radiant shapes of sleep
From one whose dreams are paradise,
Fly, when the fond wretch wakes to weep,
And day peers forth with her blank eyes ;
So fleet, so faint, so fair,
The Powers of earth and air
Fled from the folding-star of Bethlehem :
Apollo, Pan, and Love,
And even Olympian Jove,
Grew weak, for killing Truth had glared on them.
Our hills, and seas, and streams,
Dispeopled of their dreams,
Their waters turned to blood, their dew to tears,
Wailed for the golden years."

Shelley has concentrated within a few lines, put
into the mouth of the Semichorus, his thoughts of
the Greeks, and the immortality of their renown :—

" Temples and towers,
Citadels and marts, and they
Who live and die there, have been ours,
And may be thine, and must decay ;
But Greece and her foundations are
Built below the tide of war,
Based on the crystalline sea
Of thought and its eternity ;
Her citizens, imperial spirits,
Rule the present from the past,
On all this world of men inherits
Their seal is set."

Hellas is the canonisation of a race. It is the

expression in "words that breathe and thoughts that burn" of the inextinguishable admiration and affection of a poet for a people the most illustrious in arts, literature, and civilisation that the world has ever seen.

V.

THE POETRY OF SHELLEY—*Concluded.*

"He is made one with Nature : there is heard
　His voice in all her music, from the moan
　Of thunder, to the song of night's sweet bird ;
　He is a presence to be felt and known
　In darkness and in light, from herb and stone,
　Spreading itself where'er that Power may move ·
　Which has withdrawn his being to its own ;
　Which wields the world with never-wearied love,
Sustains it from beneath, and kindles it above."

Adonais.

V.

THE POETRY OF SHELLEY—*Concluded.*

In connection with Shelley and his poetry, something still remains to be said; though when all has been uttered, a subject so richly suggestive must continue unexhausted. That the poet too frequently misapprehended his own capacity is proved by the tragedy of *The Cenci*. Here we have his only attempt in the pure, unmixed dramatic form, and in scarcely anything was Shelley more successful. The works which gave him most satisfaction to contemplate are those which posterity does not regard with general favour, chiefly for the reason that they are as far from its complete understanding as the Eleusinian mysteries; while this tragedy, which Shelley entered upon with so much distrust in his own powers, remains one of the most durable monuments of his genius. Its diction is noble, though its incident is limited. It is more dramatic than

any work by Lord Byron, for the latter poet was
himself all too conspicuous in his creations,—Man-
fred, Cain, and the rest of his gallery of striking
and powerful portraits.   Shelley, on the contrary,
gives us the Cencis severally as they might have
lived.   Especially is the character of Beatrice
elaborated with a skill worthy of the great masters
of the dramatic art.   The poet depicts vividly all
the stages of feeling towards her guilty father,
through which she passed, down to the sublime
attitude of resignation before her execution.   The
full details of the terrible story of the Cenci family
are unutterable.   Shelley has taken them, and has
worked by suggestion; in his tragedy there is
nothing to offend the sensibility, and yet the black
and bloody story is charged with horror in the vigorous and nervous language of the poet.   That profusion of imagery which distinguishes most of Shelley's
lengthier poems is greatly subdued in *The Cenci ;*
the author has rightly deemed it of more importance for dramatic purposes that the imaginative
and the descriptive should not predominate over
the delineation of the passions; and in the fifth
act he exclusively depends upon the simple expression of the emotions, and the native pathos
and tragic grandeur of the situations.   Hence his
undoubted triumph, the drama being justly re-

garded as one of the greatest efforts since the time of Shakspeare. There are those, doubtless, who think that Shelley was unwise in selecting so repulsive a story for dramatic treatment; but he has answered this objection when he observes that " the highest moral purpose aimed at in the highest species of the drama is the teaching of the human heart, through its sympathies and antipathies, the knowledge of itself; in proportion to the possession of which knowledge, every human being is just, wise, sincere, tolerant, and kind. No person can be truly dishonoured by the act of another." It is scarcely possible to conceive that a perusal of *The Cenci* would lead any mind from a course of equity and goodness; on the contrary, an intense reflex light is cast upon these virtues by the very horrors which a contemplation of their opposites engenders. In the hands of some writers, such a subject might have been perilous: Shelley has not only encountered the ordeal, but has triumphed over it. Of all the passages representing the conflict of human sensation and passion in this drama, perhaps the following, which occurs towards the close of the fifth act, deserves to be best remembered :—

" *Beatrice.*   Worse than despair,
Worse than the bitterness of death, is hope :

It is the only ill which can find place
Upon the giddy, sharp, and narrow hour
Tottering beneath us.   Plead with the swift frost
That it should spare the eldest flower of spring :
Plead with awakening earthquake, o'er whose couch
Even now a city stands, strong, fair, and free ;
Now stench and blackness yawn, like death.   O, plead
With famine, or wind-walking pestilence,
Blind lightning, or the deaf sea ;—not with man !
Cruel, cold, formal man ; righteous in words,
In deeds a Cain ! No, mother, we must die :
Since such is the reward of innocent lives,
Such the alleviation of worst wrongs.
And, whilst our murderers live, and hard, cold men,
Smiling and slow, walk through a world of tears
To death as to life's sleep, 'twere just the grave
Were some strange joy for us.   Come, obscure Death,
And wind me in thine all-embracing arms !
Like a fond mother, hide me in thy bosom,
And rock me to the sleep from which none wake.
Live ye, who live, subject to one another,
As we were once, who now—

                              BERNARDO *rushes in.*

" *Bernardo.*   O, horrible !
That tears, that looks, that hope poured forth in prayer,
Even till the heart is vacant and despairs,
Should all be vain ! The ministers of death
Are waiting round the doors.   I thought I saw
Blood on the face of one—what if 'twere fancy ?
Soon the heart's blood of all I love on earth
Will sprinkle him, and he will wipe it off
As if 'twere only rain.   O life ! O world !

Cover me ! let me be no more !   To see
That perfect mirror of pure innocence
Wherein I gazed, and grew happy and good,
Shivered to dust !   To see thee, Beatrice,
Who made all lovely thou didst look upon—
Thee, light of life—dead, dark ! while I say, sister,
To hear I have no sister ; and thou, mother,
Whose love was as a bond to all our loves—
Dead !   The sweet bond broken."

One of the finest things also, in a dramatic sense, is that second scene of the fifth act, between the Judges, Beatrice, and her accuser Marzio, the assassin.   The speech of Beatrice is eloquent and impassioned, but it excites our admiration in yet a superior degree by reason of its effect.   Tenacious of life, with all the young and the beautiful, and afraid of the infamy, as well as the act of death, under circumstances so horrible, Beatrice thus pleads with her accomplice :—

" Oh, thou who tremblest on the giddy verge
Of life and death, pause ere thou answerest me ;
So mayst thou answer God with less dismay :
What evil have we done thee ?   I, alas !
Have lived but on this earth a few sad years,
And so my lot was ordered, that a father
First turned the moments of awakening life
To drops, each poisoning youth's sweet hope ; and then
Stabbed with one blow my everlasting soul,
And my untainted fame ; and even that peace

Which sleeps within the core of the heart's heart.
But the wound was not mortal; so my hate
Became the only worship I could lift
To my great Father, who in pity and love,
Armed thee, as thou dost say, to cut him off;
And thus his wrong becomes my accusation:
And art thou the accuser?   If thou hopest
Mercy in heaven show justice upon earth:
Worse than a bloody hand is a hard heart.
If thou hast done murders, made thy life's path
Over the trampled laws of God and man,
Rush not before thy Judge, and say; 'My Maker,
I have done this and more, for there was one
Who was most pure and innocent on earth;
And because she endured what never any,
Guilty or innocent, endured before;
Because her wrongs could not be told, nor thought;
Because thy hand at length did rescue her;
I with my words killed her and all her kin.'
Think, I adjure you, what it is to slay
The reverence living in the minds of men
Towards our ancient house, and stainless fame!
Think what it is to strangle infant pity
Cradled in the belief of guileless looks,
Till it become a crime to suffer.   Think
What 'tis to blot with infamy and blood,
All that which shows like innocence, and is,—
Hear me, great God!   I swear, most innocent,—
So that the world lose all discrimination
Between the sly, fierce, wild regard of guilt,
And that which now compels thee to reply
To what I ask: Am I, or am I not,
A parricide?"

The appeal is irresistible: mark the triumph which the poet has achieved by it in an artistic sense. In previous scenes were witnessed the conspiracy between Beatrice and the assassins, the murder of the Count, and the rewards heaped by his daughter upon the murderers. In the Hall of Justice the bloody story is unfolded; Marzio is conscious of his doom; therefore, he has no reason for sparing those who were implicated in the tragedy. Yet so powerful is Beatrice's appeal, even upon the mind of one so base that he has executed crimes merely for the sake of material gain, that he cries out before the Judges he alone is guilty: those whom he previously accused are innocent. Tortures are applied; but the memory of Beatrice's appeal is so vivid that he adheres to his assertion of her innocence when upon the wheel, smiles upon the officers of justice, and, holding his breath, dies with his secret stubbornly preserved. This scene, as I have said, is eminently powerful and dramatic: it will favourably compare with some of the best passages in the Elizabethan dramatists.

Naturally, Shelley was a man of a pleasant humour, but that which might have become in him a grateful and delectable stream was early turned into a river of gall. In personal intercourse he

had the sense of humour, and his own observations
were frequently enlivened by a nimble wit, but in
his writings this quality changes into fierce invective and the bitterest satire. His disappoint-
ments, and the cruel treatment he received at the
hands of others, begat in him what we cannot but
regard as an unhealthy condition of mind. This
did not last through his career, but it embittered
many of his best years, and cramped his energies
in the noblest fields of poetic enterprise. While
under the sway of a heart bleeding from wrong and
injustice, he penned that portion of his writings
which may be designated as the satiric. Through
this vehicle it was that he, whose philosophy
for the recovery of mankind was love, sent forth
blazing curses upon his enemies. He believed in
no hell, and yet all the reputed tortures of the
damned pale before those he calls down upon Lord
Castlereagh and Lord Chancellor Eldon. Wit
becomes a burning lava, which he pours forth from
an apparently inexhaustible supply. The man
who wrote that part of *Peter Bell the Third* com-
mencing "Hell is a city much like London," was
in no humorous or even cynical mood. He had
almost lost his faith in the virtue of mankind. It
is, however, necessary that there should be no
misconception with regard to this poem. It was

vulgarly supposed, and the error is not yet
completely exorcised, that Shelley intended a
severe personal attack upon Wordsworth, under
the cognomen of Peter, and nothing more, by the
work. But while he certainly desired to express
his sense of what he considered to be Wordsworth's
time-serving character, he cherished a very high
opinion of his poetry, and by Peter Bell, he intended to depict the pitiable state of any man who
gives way to constant tergiversation—especially the
man whose changes of opinion result in material
advantage. Shelley deeply regretted that he
should only be able to compare Wordsworth, "the
most natural and tender of lyric poets" (to use his
own phrase) with "Simonides, that flatterer of the
Sicilian tyrants." Under the influence of this
feeling he wrote *Peter Bell*, intending, nevertheless,
that it should bear with it and convey the most
general signification. The only passage, perhaps,
of the poem which approaches real humour (the
rest being too deeply satiric to be thus described)
is that detailing how the disease of dulness overtook Peter, and infected everything in connection
with him :—

> " Peter was dull—he was at first
>   Dull—O, so dull, so very dull !
> Whether he talked, wrote, or rehearsed,

Still with this dulness was he cursed—
    Dull ; beyond all conception, dull.

" No one could read his books—no mortal,
    But a few natural friends, would hear him ;
The parson came not near his portal ;
His state was like that of the immortal
    Described by Swift—no man could bear him.

" A printer's boy, folding those pages,
    Fell slumbrously upon one side ;
Like those famed seven who slept three ages.
To wakeful frenzy's vigil rages,
    As opiates, were the same applied.

" Even the reviewers who were hired
    To do the work of his reviewing,
With adamantine nerves, grew tired ;—
Gaping and torpid they retired,
    To dream of what they should be doing."

The contagion spread beyond all power of suppression. Peter's servant maids, dogs, and sportive kitten, grew somnolent; every cottager yawned upon his neighbour; asses refused to bray, and no little cur cocked up his ears; within the space of seven miles no bailiff dared to enter a house lest he should bear upon his face for fifteen months the yawn of such a venture. The whole thing is well done; and there can be no doubt that some portions of Wordsworth's poetry, which readily lend themselves to burlesque, suggested this travesty. But whenever Shelley devotes himself to the witty or the humorous, he gives us either the grotesque, as in *Swellfoot the Tyrant*, or the fiercely satiric, as in the *Masque of Anarchy*, and several of his personal miscellaneous poems. Whatever interest these efforts may possess, however (and there are lines in the *Masque of Anarchy* equal to almost anything that Shelley has written) they do not contribute to the ground-work of his fame. Some of them we could well do without —they contain no evidence of that mission it is the poet's office to unfold; and I am no believer in the chimera that every line which a man of genius has written must necessarily be valuable. Political poems can be written by individuals who are not poets, and while Shelley is deserving of every justification which can be advanced—when we call to remembrance the deep provocations which drew forth these outbursts of indignation—the poet of *Adonais* and *Prometheus* is a being of a far loftier type than the castigator of an infamous British minister.

As the poet of Nature, Shelley challenges the warmest eulogy. He possesses so many other claims upon us, that we are apt to forget he has no modern rival save Wordsworth in the intensity of his natural vision. The moods and manifesta-

tions of nature were to him as an open book, and
the passages which could be culled from his works
in support of this are infinite in number, and
endless in variety and beauty. He enjoyed the
empire over nature as well as that of humanity.
Lord of the earth, the sea, and the sky, the
numberless forms of beauty peculiar to each
element fed his spirit with love and all spiritual
thoughts. The lark in the firmament; the flower
which bursts into loveliness by the wayside; the
cloud which flits restlessly in the heavens; the
wave which sobs out its strength upon the pathless
and impenetrable shore—spoke to him as they
spoke to the great poet with whom I have compared
him. He counted not his days by the calendars
of men, but by the calendars of nature. Nothing
existed that to him was not a minister of grace.

Unrivalled we know him to have been in the
justness and extent of his observations on natural
objects; and though he accumulated little scientific knowledge, " he knew every plant by its name,
and was familiar with the history and habits of
every production of the earth; he could inter-
pret without a fault each appearance in the
sky : and the varied phenomena of heaven and
earth filled him with deep emotion." There has
probably been no poet who, considering the

brevity of his life, spent so much time in the open air; he revelled in the changeful aspects of nature, and his communings with her spirit filled him with a joy far deeper than that he drew from contact with human kind. It is a mistake to suppose that the most divinely gifted poet has found himself sufficient to the highest tasks by the aid of his inspiration alone; he who would prove he is a poet must not only love but study and understand nature. He must be perfectly acquainted with her, in her manifold aspects. Every lyric of Shelley's shows him to have been a singer of this character. The Æolian harp of the woods, and the moans and struggles of the tempestuous ocean, had for him no clearer or more articulate utterance than the meanest and most diminutive objects in animate or inanimate nature. The joyous skylark, high in air, filled him with exquisite soul music,—

> " Better than all measures
>   Of delightful sound,
>   Better than all treasures
>   That in books are found,
> Thy skill to poet were, thou scorner of the ground !
>
>   " Teach me half the gladness
>   That thy brain must know,
>   Such harmonious madness
>   From my lips would flow,
> The world should listen then, as I am listening now."

Mingled emotions succeed, as he wails forth a
dirge for the dying year; but even here there are
indications of that intense joy which nature fore-
shadows in her darkest hour, and will inevitably
bring to pass,—

> " Orphan hours, the year is dead,
> 　　Come and sigh, come and weep !
> Merry hours, smile instead,
> 　　For the year is but asleep :
> See, it smiles as it is sleeping,
> Mocking your untimely weeping.
>
> " As an earthquake rocks a corse
> 　　In its coffin in the clay,
> So white Winter, that rough nurse,
> 　　Rocks the dead-cold year to-day ;
> Solemn hours ! wail aloud
> For your mother in her shroud.
>
> " As the wild air stirs and sways
> 　　The tree-swung cradle of a child,
> So the breath of these rude days
> 　　Rocks the year :—be calm and mild,
> Trembling hours ; she will arise
> With new love within her eyes.
>
> " January grey is here,
> 　　Like a sexton by her grave ;
> February bears the bier,
> 　　March with grief doth howl and rave,
> And April weeps—but, O ye hours !
> Follow with May's fairest flowers."

Let me cite a few passages from the poems of Shelley which will prove his acquaintance with, and power to depict, the varying phases of nature. Discarding his lengthier works, which will not so readily yield the extracts we need, but which are nevertheless charged with the same elements, take one of the early poems, " A Summer Evening in the Churchyard of Lechlade, Gloucestershire,"— and see what a picture is furnished of the descending twilight :—

" The wind has swept from the wide atmosphere
   Each vapour that obscured the sunset's ray ;
And pallid evening twines its beaming hair
   In duskier braids around the languid eyes of day :
Silence and twilight, unbeloved of men,
Creep hand in hand from yon obscurest glen.

" They breathe their spells towards the departing day,
   Encompassing the earth, air, stars, and sea ;
Light, sound, and motion own the potent sway,
   Responding to the charm with its own mystery.
The winds are still, or the dry church-tower grass
Knows not their gentle motions as they pass.

" Thou too, aërial Pile ! whose pinnacles
   Point from one shrine like pyramids of fire,
Obeyest in silence their sweet solemn spells,
   Clothing in hues of heaven thy dim and distant spire,
Around whose lessening and invisible height
Gather among the stars the clouds of night.

" The dead are sleeping in their sepulchres ; .
  And, mouldering as they sleep, a thrilling sound,
Half sense, half thought, among the darkness stirs,
  Breathed from their wormy beds all living things around,
And mingling with the still night and mute sky
Its awful hush is felt inaudibly.

" Thus solemnised and softened, death is mild
  And terrorless as this serenest night :
Here could I hope, like some inquiring child
  Sporting on graves, that death did hide from human sight
Sweet secrets, or beside its breathless sleep
That loveliest dreams perpetual watch did keep."

The mastery of Shelley, in this and in other
poems, is shown in his capacity to infuse the reader
with feelings similar to those originally felt by the
poet—similar in kind, if not in intensity.   The
scene and the churchyard of Lechlade, and that particular evening when Shelley conceived his stanzas,
are all presented vividly to the reader.   Witness,
again, the lines on Mont Blanc, which challenge
comparison with the similar poem by Coleridge :
the latter has probably the advantage of sublimity,
but Shelley once more demonstrates his superiority
in imitating the very aspects and operations of
nature.   The mountain speaks to him of things
multitudinous, of remoter worlds, of dark and stolid
power, of the earthquake, of the mortality of man,
and the immutability of nature.   As it rears its

mighty head before him in silent majesty, Mont
Blanc has a lesson and a reflection for the poet :—

" Mont Blanc yet gleams on high : the power is there,
   The still and solemn power of many sights
   And many sounds, and much of life and death.
   In the calm darkness of the moonless nights,
   In the lone glare of day, the snows descend
   Upon that Mountain ; none beholds them there,
   Nor when the flakes burn in the sinking sun, .
   Or the star-beams dart through them : winds contend
   Silently there, and heap the snow, with breath
   Rapid and strong, but silently ! Its home
   The voiceless lightning in these solitudes
   Keeps innocently, and like vapour broods
   Over the snow. The secret strength of things,
   Which governs thought, and to the infinite dome
   Of heaven is as a law, inhabits thee !
   And what were thou, and earth, and stars, and sea,
   If to the human mind's imaginings
   Silence and solitude were vacancy ? "

How fine, in its merely descriptive aspect, and the
richness of its colour, is the following passage from
the " Lines written among the Euganean Hills ! "

   " Beneath is spread like a green sea
      The waveless plain of Lombardy,
      Bounded by the vaporous air,
      Islanded by cities fair ;
      Underneath day's azure eyes,
      Ocean's nursling, Venice lies,—
      A peopled labyrinth of walls,

Amphitrite's destined halls,
Which her hoary sire now paves
With his blue and beaming waves.
Lo ! the sun upsprings behind,
Broad, red, radiant, half-reclined
On the level quivering line
Of the waters crystalline ;
And before that chasm of light,
As within a furnace bright,
Column, tower, and dome, and spire,
Shine like obelisks of fire,
Pointing with inconstant motion
From the altar of dark ocean
To the sapphire-tinted skies ;
As the flames of sacrifice
From the marbled shrines did rise
As to pierce the dome of gold
Where Apollo spoke of old.

" Sun-girt City ! thou hast been
Ocean's child, and then his queen ;
Now is come a darker day,
And thou soon must be his prey,
If the power that raised thee here
Hallow so thy watery bier.
A less drear ruin then than now,
With thy conquest-branded brow
Stooping to the slave of slaves
From thy throne among the waves,
Wilt thou be, when the sea-mew
Flies as once before it flew,
O'er thine isles depopulate,
And all is in its ancient state,

> Save where many a palace-gate
> With green sea-flowers overgrown
> Like a rock of ocean's own,
> Topples o'er the abandon'd sea
> As the tides change sullenly.
> The fisher on his watery way,
> Wandering at the close of day,
> Will spread his sail and seize his oar,
> Till he pass the gloomy shore,
> Lest thy dead should, from their sleep
> Bursting o'er the starlight deep,
> Lead a rapid masque of death
> O'er the waters of his path."

Here is also an exceedingly majestic image, drawn from the same poem :—

> " Lo, the sun floats up the sky,
> Like thought-winged Liberty,
> Till the universal light
> Seems to level plain and height ;
> From the sea a mist has spread,
> And the beams of morn lie dead
> On the towers of Venice now,
> Like its glory long ago."

Occasionally, within the compass of a few lines, Shelley paints a landscape as completely as the more extended labours of the conscientious artist could produce it for us. This is a picture of such a character, a fragment, which the poet entitles *The Isle* :—

> " There was a little lawny islet
> By anemone and violet,
> 　　　Like mosaic, paven ;
> And its roof was flowers and leaves
> Which the summer's breath enweaves,
> Where nor sun nor showers nor breeze
> Pierce the pines and tallest trees,
> 　　　Each a gem engraven.
> Girt by many an azure wave
> With which the clouds and mountains pave
> 　　　A lake's blue chasm."

The same felicity and power are displayed, combined with the presentation of a remarkable image, in the succeeding lines upon the waning moon :—

> " And like a dying lady, lean and pale,
> Who totters forth, wrapt in a gauzy veil,
> Out of her chamber, led by the insane
> And feeble wanderings of her fading brain,
> The moon arose up in the murky East,
> A white and shapeless mass."

Not even the minutest additional stroke is requisite to enable the mind to grasp this true and powerful figure. On other occasions Shelley's poetry is noticeable for revealing the influence of nature upon the sentiments and emotions. He probably never was happier in exhibiting the singular harmony and relation between outward nature and the inner feeling and emotion, than in the *Stanzas, written in dejection, near Naples.* In

these lines is perceived the mind when under the
subtle operation of exterior influences—

" The sun is warm, the sky is clear,
 The waves are dancing fast and bright,
Blue isles and snowy mountains wear
 The purple noon's transparent might ;
The breath of the moist earth is light,
 Around its unexpanded buds ;
Like many a voice of one delight,
 The winds, the birds, the ocean floods,
The City's voice itself is soft like Solitude's.

" I see the Deep's untrampled floor
 With green and purple sea-weeds strown ;
I see the waves upon the shore,
 Like light dissolved in star-showers, thrown :
I sit upon the sands alone,
 The lightning of the noon-tide ocean
Is flashing round me, and a tone
 Arises from its measured motion,
How sweet ! did any heart now share in my emotion.

 .   .   .   .   .

" Some might lament that I were cold,
 As I when this sweet day is gone,
Which my lost heart, too soon grown old,
 Insults with this untimely moan ;
They might lament—for I am one
 Whom men love not—and yet regret,
Unlike this day, which, when the sun
 Shall on its stainless glory set,
Will linger, though enjoyed, like joy in memory yet."

At the risk of citing a lyric familiar in the mouths
of readers as any lyric by any poet, it is impossible
in speaking of Shelley as an interpreter of nature,
to omit mention of *The Cloud.* The poem is more
than exquisite amongst the exquisitely beautiful ;
it is unique. The English language, probably,
does not present its equal for music, metaphor,
and full and untrammelled expression. Where
every stanza is so rich in melody, it is difficult
to confer upon any the distinction of being the
best. The first and last are most frequently
quoted and applauded ; but, if compelled to select,
I should say that Shelley reached his highest
elevation, in the poetic sense, in the third and
fourth. These latter stanzas, with the concluding one, must be given as an additional evidence
of the poet's wonderful perception of nature, and
his power of felicitous comparison—

" The sanguine sunrise, with his meteor eyes,
    And his burning plumes outspread,
Leaps on the back of my sailing rack,
    When the morning star shines dead.
As on the jag of a mountain crag,
    Which an earthquake rocks and swings,
An eagle alit one moment may sit
    In the light of its golden wings.
And when sunset may breathe, from the lit sea beneath,
    Its ardours of rest and of love,

And the crimson pall of eve may fall
    From the depth of heaven above,
With wings folded I rest, on mine airy nest,
    As still as a brooding dove.

" That orbèd maiden, with white fire laden,
    Whom mortals call the moon,
Glides glimmering o'er my fleece-like floor,
    By the midnight breezes strewn ;
And wherever the beat of her unseen feet,
    Which only the angels hear,
May have broken the woof of my tent's thin roof,
    The stars peep behind her and peer ;
And I laugh to see them whirl and flee,
    Like a swarm of golden bees,
When I widen the rent in my wind-built tent,
    Till the calm rivers, lakes, and seas,
Like strips of the sky fallen through me on high,
    Are each paved with the moon and these.

.   .   .   .   .   .

" I am the daughter of earth and water,
    And the nursling of the sky :
I pass through the pores of the ocean and shores ;
    I change, but I cannot die.
For after the rain, when with never a stain,
    The pavilion of heaven is bare,
And the winds and sunbeams with their convex gleams,
    Build up the blue dome of air,
I silently laugh at my own cenotaph,
    And out of the caverns of rain,
Like a child from the womb, like a ghost from the tomb,
    I arise and unbuild it again."

R

It would be possible to linger over each page of
Shelley, and discover in it some references to the
beauty or grandeur of this ever-changing nature,
and to the endless variety of atmospheric phenomena. Nature and the elements are the warp
and woof of his poetry. How we see a comming-
ling of both in these stanzas on *Summer and
Winter !*—

> " It was a bright and cheerful afternoon,
> Towards the end of the sunny month of June,
> When the north wind congregates in crowds
> The floating mountains of the silver clouds
> From the horizon—and the stainless sky
> Opens beyond them like eternity.
> All things rejoiced beneath the sun, the weeds,
> The river, and the corn-fields, and the reeds ;
> The willow leaves that glanced in the light breeze,
> And the firm foliage of the larger trees.

> " It was a winter such as when birds die
> In the deep forests ; and the fishes lie
> Stiffened in the translucent ice, which makes
> Even the mud and slime of the warm lakes
> A wrinkled clod, as hard as brick ; and when,
> Among their children, comfortable men
> Gather about great fires, and yet feel cold :
> Alas ! then for the homeless beggar old ! "

To equal Shelley's dirge for Autumn, we must go
back to the older poets. The modern have not
rivalled it in simplicity and intensity, nor yet in

that striking element of personification which is
so characteristic of Shelley—

" The warm sun is failing, the bleak wind is wailing,
The bare boughs are sighing, the pale flowers are dying,
   And the year
On the earth her death-bed, in a shroud of leaves dead,
    Is lying ;
   Come, months, come away,
   From November to May,
   In your saddest array ;
   Follow the bier
   Of the dead cold year,
And like dim shadows watch by her sepulchre.

" The chill rain is falling, the nipt worm is crawling,
The rivers are swelling, the thunder is knelling
   For the year ;
The blithe swallows are flown, and the lizards each gone
   To his dwelling ;
   Come, months, come away ;
   Put on white, black, and gray,
   Let your light sisters play—
   Ye, follow the bier
   Of the dead cold year,
And make her grave green with tear on tear."

It is in Shelley's poetry that we find his true
biography. What life had he—life, that is, in its
largest, fullest sense—apart from his poetic visions
and aspirations ? Shelley is a vague and shadowy
being till we study his poetry and become per-

meated with his spirit. In proportion as we understand his work, do we attain knowledge of his
humanity. Mr. Browning, in defining what he
regards as Shelley's highest and most predomi-
nating characteristic, calls it "his simultaneous
perception of power and love in the absolute; and
of beauty and good in the concrete; while he
throws from his poet's station, between both,
swifter, subtler, and more numerous films, for the
connection of each with each, than have been
thrown by any modern artificer of whom I have
knowledge." The justness and accuracy of these
distinctions may be tested by a consideration of
such fascinating and noble poems as *The Triumph
of Life*, the *Hymn to Intellectual Beauty*, and the
Ode to the West Wind. Shelley is here at his best,
when his crude philosophy no longer obtrudes
itself, and he is content with the simple exercise
of the imagination. His pure imaginative gifts
were superior to those of either Byron or Wordsworth; and, like the latter, he had comparative
command of his genius—though he could not, with
the author of the *Excursion*, subdue the personal
to the universal. It has been well said of Shelley
that in poems with a political vein "he had the use
of the left hand only." As I have before intimated,
he was a destroyer and not a builder, politically

and socially. Shelley's refined intellect mistook its office in giving his political opinions through a poetic medium; and the harmony of his work was destroyed by convulsions of anger at what he deemed the violation of the eternal principles of right. It is in his perception of the beautiful, his sympathy, his grand enthusiasm, his eloquence, and his imagination, that his strength lies. He lacked the philosophic calm of Plato and the towering invention of the great Elizabethan poets. His life and his poetry are a record of ecstatic passion and spiritual unrest. Yet after all deductions, he will exercise a more durable influence upon the poetry of England than any of his contemporaries and successors save Wordsworth. His bays cannot wither with the lapse of time. Other poets may have their seasons of spasmodic popularity, but he can never be superseded. With twenty years added to his career, his hand might have touched that of Shakspeare.

And now to gather up the threads of this criticism. In addition to those aspects in which we have regarded him, Shelley stands confessed a consummate master of lyrical verse—the greatest lyric poet of the nineteenth century. And lyric poetry, it should ever be remembered, bears a serious import and purpose, besides that of ministering to the delight of men. Were such not the case how could we legitimately assign to this writer that position which is now universally conceded to him? The poet is greater as a teacher than the man of science, because of his capacity to speak to all men, and his one organ of speech is effective in reaching all. He discovers that which is of interest to humanity, and unfolds it. It is the faculty of discovering hidden analogies, combined with the power of expressing them artistically and musically, which makes the poet. Nations have in every epoch throbbed with the desire for liberty; all men have observed the clouds which veil the midnight sky; sunset and sunrise are every-day occurrences; the daisy has bloomed for centuries; the bird has carolled in the sky for unnumbered ages—yet to ordinary men all these things bear no second meaning behind their palpable existence as facts and things. But the poet, the immortal singer, fills other men with that enthusiastic love for freedom which consumes himself; he deduces lessons from the passage of the midnight clouds across the heavens, and finds new links between nature, man, and the Deity, in the song of the bird, the upturned face of the daisy, and the crimson robes in which the sun is arrayed as he goes forth upon his triumphant career. In this view of the bard, who is a worthier votary in the great temple of poesy than Shelley, whose soul overflowed with love and sympathy, whose mind was ever open to the endless forms of beauty in the universe, and whose heart yearned for the emancipation of humanity from vice and error? His hopes and his inextinguishable desires find expression in the lines which he addresses to the West Wind—

" Make me thy lyre, even as the forest is ;
    What if my leaves are falling like its own ?
    The tumult of thy mighty harmonies

" Will take from both a deep autumnal tone,
    Sweet though in sadness.   Be thou, spirit fierce,
    My spirit ! Be thou me, impetuous one !

" Drive my dead thoughts over the universe
    Like withered leaves to quicken a new birth ;
    And, by the incantation of this verse,

" Scatter, as from an unextinguished hearth
    Ashes and sparks, my words among mankind !
    Be through my lips to unawakened earth

" The trumpet of a prophecy ! O wind,
    If Winter comes, can Spring be far behind ?"

Who shall say that Shelley has not been "the trumpet of a prophecy ?" What matters it, though some of his poems should be disfigured by affectation, and others by a quixotic assault upon

windmills of his own creation?—there is yet a
glamour over all his song, which proclaims him
the great poet.   Even in his translations—an
important branch of his art—the same glamour
shines.   We understand the old aphorism, *poeta
nascitur, non fit*, when it is applied to him.   The
value and extent of his work, when placed in juxta-
position with the brevity of his life, leave us but
astonishment and wonder.   He was inspired, and
has since been the source of inspiration in others.
It is little to say that his melody is superior to that
of any other modern poet.   He divides the lyric
crown with Burns.   The latter is a poet of universal
sympathies, and in that respect takes precedence
of Shelley, but the author of *The Cloud* transcends
even the poet-king of the north in simple music.
His lyrical endowment was also accompanied by
passion and earnestness.   His sincerity cannot be
denied, nor his rigid adherence to what, in his
seer's vision, he deemed to be the truth.   He sang
of things old and new, and justified his title to the
appellation of bard by the new fire which he
struck out of the expiring ashes of the past.
Nothing in nature appeared ugly or discordant to
him; and had his faith in humanity equalled his
reverence for the Spirit that breathes through all
things, he would, by an extension of his brief

span of life, have taken rank with the greatest of our poets. The day for which he longed with all the ardour of his passionate nature was as yet unborn—sleeping in the womb of Time—a day when men should be knit together by the sacred ties of benevolence and love. His prophetic eyes shone with a glorified light from other suns than ours. Imperfect as the rest of humanity, and yet waging ceaselessly the conflict with evil, the Eternal Voice which speaks to all—but to many fruitlessly and in vain—thrilled him to the very springs of his being. His soul was one with all things: it embraced the outcast of the world, and the children of light; the grandeur and minutiæ of the material universe; the majestic creations of mythology; and the human Prometheus struggling with woe and wrong. He was the sweet singer of his age, destined to live in the reverent affection of all succeeding ages; for out of the burning depths of his soul sprang immortal music in praise of love, beauty, and virtue.